# *Free Fall*

# FREE FALL

## Elite Ops #3

## EMMY CURTIS

FOREVER YOURS

New York   Boston

Copyright © 2018 by Emmy Curtis

Cover design by Elizabeth Turner Stokes
Cover copyright © 2018 by Hachette Book Group, Inc.

Forever Yours
Hachette Book Group
1290 Avenue of the Americas, New York, NY 10104
forever-romance.com
twitter.com/foreverromance

First published as an ebook and as a print on demand: July 2018

Forever Yours is an imprint of Grand Central Publishing. The Forever Yours name and logo are trademarks of Hachette Book Group, Inc.

The publisher is not responsible for websites (or their content) that are not owned by the publisher.

The Hachette Speakers Bureau provides a wide range of authors for speaking events. To find out more, go to www.hachettespeakersbureau.com or call (866) 376-6591.

ISBNs: 978-1-4789-4796-7 (ebook), 978-1-4789-4798-1 (print-on-demand trade paperback)

*For the chief of my heart:*
*thank you for the best decade of my life.*

*Free Fall*

# CHAPTER 1

Colonel Duke Cameron wasn't the squared-away commander everybody saw. He wasn't the obedient by-the-books officer he'd accidentally become.

But that was going to change. Right now.

Two pilots were missing—on his watch. And it didn't matter that the military had farmed out these Red Flag training games in the Nevada desert to a huge tech corporation this year. It didn't matter that he had only two years to go before he hit the minimum retirement length of service if he just kept his head down and played by the rules.

It *did* matter that he now had only one hour before he was supposed to meet with Casey Jacobs. They'd encountered each other a couple of times when he'd been deployed—once flying MJ-130Js in Germany, another couple of times in Afghanistan. Now she worked for TechGen-One, the third-party military contractor sponsoring these training exercises for the most elite pilots around the world.

When Casey had come to his office that afternoon, she looked as beautiful and sharp as usual, but there had been an imperceptible barrier between them. He was sure she knew something about the crash, and why her company was taking forever to find the aircraft and the pilots.

He told himself, again, that this meeting had nothing to do with the looks they had exchanged when they'd crossed paths in Kabul. Nothing to do with the time they'd taken shelter in the same bunker when their base had been attacked by insurgents. Nothing to do with how she'd been his "what if" person. Nope. Nada. Never.

Casey Jacobs had her phone in her hand and was pacing the length of her hotel room. She should switch the phone off, right? But maybe TGO would get suspicious if she did. Her brain was jumping from thought to thought. She had to calm down.

She took some deep breaths and sat on the bed. Then after a couple of seconds, she put the phone in the drawer of the bedside table. It would be better if it rang and she didn't hear it. Less suspicious maybe. Easier on her nerves, at least.

All she'd done was make an innocent inquiry to head office about the equipment on the planes that had crashed, and her world had collapsed around her. If she kept her mouth shut, everything would be okay. Maybe.

Her work-buddy Malcolm, at TGO's headquarters, had warned her off. Suggested that TGO tapped its employees' phones. Suggested that they sued people who asked too many questions. Suggested that when TGO whistle-blowers committed suicide, that maybe it wasn't exactly suicide. *What the hell had she gotten into?* She couldn't begin to fathom what had happened to her life in the previous twenty-four hours.

But if TGO had tapped her phone, they would have already heard her panicked message. *Malcolm! What's going on? We have planes and pilots missing, and their last transmissions suggested they were experiencing the same bugs we reported in our PreCall software last year. Aircraft overcorrecting, lack of pilot control, radio static. Did we put PreCall on their aircraft? Did they even know? Is that legal? Call me back!*

Even if she didn't have specific knowledge of any wrongdoing, she already sensed that her new company—and her new boss, Mr. Danvers—were somehow above the law. The company letterhead boasted names from the U.S. Senate and the House of Representatives. From high up in the Pentagon. From the West Wing of the White House.

She had to try persuade them that she was on board with the company line. But her military training—her honor and integrity—were battling against her survival instinct. She just plain didn't know what to do.

After her panicked message to Malcolm, he'd sent her a newspaper clipping about how her company had won a lawsuit against a man named James Turner, who had leaked information to a journalist. The judgment had left Turner close to destitute. No one had raised an eyebrow when he'd killed himself. Except now, Casey had been given reason to wonder. Malcom had suggested to her that TGO had ruined him as a message to other whistle-blowers, and then killed him to stop him from talking.

But things like that just didn't happen in real life. Did they? She'd known only the air force before she joined TGO. What did she know? Her heart started racing again. Could one company do that? Surely not. Unless the company was stacked with former military and former CIA types. And they thought they were at risk. And the company's shareholders were the most powerful people in the country. She collapsed on the bed, her knees fizzing, as if she were about to pass out. Could that really happen to her?

The bedside table vibrated. When she'd taken a breath and climbed down from the ceiling, she leaned over and opened the drawer, peering in, not daring to touch the phone in case…well, she didn't really know.

The number was from Nellis Air Force Base. She frowned and slid her finger across the screen to pick up the call. "Hello?"

"Thank God you're there, baby."

She frowned, not being able to place the voice. "Who is this?"

"Really? We flew together downrange and you don't even remember me? I *saved* your *life*." He sounded hurt.

She grinned. "Animal? Is that you?" Relief threaded through her as she sat back down on the bed. The Korean air force pilot had saved her life, and the lives of her crew. He'd taken out the nest of a surface-to-air missile that had locked on to her aircraft, and then took out the missile too. He'd been laughing over the intercom as he had performed a maneuver that had seemed to defy physics as he'd blown the target to hell. Educated in America, he sometimes sounded more like a Texan than a native of Seoul.

"You know it. How've you been? I hear you defected to TGO," he said. His tone was casual, but there was something tense simmering beneath it.

Her stomach clenched again. She took a breath. "I'd never defect." She left it hanging there.

He paused. "Then I'm calling in my favor."

"What do you need?" she asked, knowing she was already in the hole. They wanted to go search for the missing pilots.

"I need you to get us off base. I hear TGO has it on lockdown," the Animal said.

Her mind started whirring, and he fell silent to let her think. "How many of you?"

"Eight, give or take."

"Can you tell me what you're planning?" she asked. And then she remembered about her phone. "Oh, wait. Don't even tell me. There isn't enough booze or women on base to satisfy the Animal?"

"Riiiight?" he said, obviously perplexed.

"Let me call you back." She hung up before he could say anything else, and picked up the phone on her bedside table. She input the number he had called from. "It's me."

"Okay. Sure you're not in the CIA instead of TGO?" the Animal said, a touch of humor in his voice.

She wished.

"I'm just being careful. As you should. Can you get a

minivan from transport and make out like you're all going out to party? I'll make sure I'm at the back gate. What time?"

"As soon as possible. It'll take me about fifteen minutes to get a van. Hold on."

She could hear him talking to someone.

"Yeah. Fifteen minutes. Let's make it twenty, I need to pick up some supplies."

"You're going into the desert, aren't you?" she asked. "You're going to look for the two pilots."

"We're going out looking for our friends." The Animal's voice was firm and unbendable. "The way we'd go look for you, if you'd crashed out there."

Tears welled up in her eyes. "I know," Casey said simply. She had no doubt about that. And if she were still in the military, she too would have busted out of lockdown to search for a missing airman.

She looked at the clock by the bed. She was due to meet Cameron in ten minutes at the officers' club. She hoped he'd wait for her.

"See you there," she told Animal.

She grabbed her bag and car keys and slipped on her sandals. She was already in the dress she'd planned on wearing on her date. No. Not a date. Would strappy sandals make it seem too much like a date? Would sneakers make her dress look stupid? Urgh. She'd grab both pairs of shoes and make up her mind in the car.

She ran down the stairs rather than waiting for the elevator and was in her car in five minutes. She drove past the officers' club on the way to the gate, just to see if Cameron was already there. If he'd been waiting for her outside, she'd have stopped to tell him she had an errand to run first. She couldn't see him, so she pressed on through the base.

When she reached the rear side of Nellis, she parked her car at the visitor center and walked over to the TGO guys manning the gate. When they saw her coming, they ran to the door of the security hut and held it open for her.

"Good evening, ma'am. What can I help you with?" the younger of the two men said.

"My friends want to go out on the town tonight, and I told them they could go." She rolled her eyes, as if totally exasperated with them.

"I'm afraid the base is on lockdown," the young guy said.

An older man looked over the top of his glasses at her. "It's okay, Scott. This is Ms. Jacobs. She's a senior VP on the board of directors. She speaks for Mr. Danvers."

The young man looked confused.

"Mr. Danvers is the CEO of TGO, Scott. You know, the company you work for?" the older man said, as if he were talking to a kid. He got off his swivel chair and came from around the high desk, shaking his head. "Can't get the staff these days."

She grinned. "We were all new once," she said.

The older man shook his head again, as if in dismay, and raised his eyebrows at her. "He's not that new," he said drily.

She grinned and handed her TGO ID to the younger security guard and signed a piece of paper on the clipboard he handed over. As she did, she realized her mistake. Her name was documented now. Danvers would know she'd let the airmen out. There was no getting away from it. She saw a minibus from the air force recreation facility headed toward the gate. It wasn't hard to figure it was them as they were literally the only vehicle exiting the base.

"Here they are," she said, trying to inject a cheeriness into her voice, when all she was feeling was doubt, bordering on fear. "I'm going to follow them out. I think it would be safer to chaperone them, and make sure they come right back on base after." She didn't know why that had slipped out, but as soon as she said it, she knew she'd feel safer off base.

She opened the door and breezed out of the security hut. Her car keys in hand, she dashed to her car and pulled in behind the minivan. She could see five heads in the government vehicle. One of them was the Animal, and she wondered who the others were.

The younger guy opened the electronic security gates. She waved to thank him, but he was looking at the old security guard, who seemed to be shouting. With a radio to his ear, the older guy slammed his hand down on the control board, and the gate started to close on her.

Adrenaline shot through her. She wasn't stopping. She needed to get out, maybe find a lawyer. Hide. She gunned the car, stomping on the gas.

A motorcyclist outfitted in black came up behind her. Nope. No way she was stopping. She took one last look at the security man, who seemed to be punching all the buttons on the gate mechanism in fury.

She accelerated through the gate as it closed, clipping a

side mirror off her car. She was free. She took a deep breath. But also, she'd just passed the point of no return. There was no talking her way out of this one.

She wondered if she should flag down the Animal to warn him, but as she went to flash her high beams at him, about eight other heads popped up from the floor of the minivan. She couldn't help but nod in approval. She would let him get on with what he was doing—the air force would protect them all against TGO.

It wouldn't protect her, though. She'd just disobeyed a direct order from her CEO. Her mind went to the elaborate contract she'd signed when she'd joined TGO. She was pretty sure she'd just broken about five clauses.

She was in the shit now.

# CHAPTER 2

Cameron had just been about to pull off his motorcycle helmet in the parking lot of the officers' club, when he'd seen Casey.

She'd slowed right down as she passed the entrance to the parking lot, then accelerated off. And the expression he'd seen on her face made him change his mind about going in to order drinks.

She'd looked tense. Lines had furrowed her brow, and her lips had been pressed firmly together as she scanned the front of the club, maybe looking for him?

Instinctively he put his helmet back on and gunned the engine. Barely even registering the decision, he peeled out of the parking lot and looked for her car.

By the time he'd caught up—and he was doing the strictly enforced base speed limit of twenty miles per hour—she was running from the security office at the gate back to her car.

Something prickled his skin as he watched the security

gate open to let a government-issue minivan leave the base. That was strange. No one had been allowed to leave the compound since TGO had taken over operational control of the base.

Casey looked as if she were heading back to the officers' club and their date, but at the last minute she swung in behind the van and followed it out. He'd been well and truly stood up.

He took a breath and was about to return to his house when he heard shouting. He looked back at the gate to see it literally closing on Casey's car. Something metallic grated and a projectile flew off her car and clanged on the pavement—a side mirror maybe?

If there wasn't a malfunction with the gate, TGO was deliberately trying to stop her from leaving. Cameron slipped his visor down and accelerated toward the gate, this time paying no mind to the speed limit.

The gate was closing faster, now that Casey's car wasn't in the way. He only had a couple of seconds before he would crash into the completely closed titanium gate. It was unsurvivable at his speed. The engine growled as it surged under his control. Time slowed as he watched the gate slide shut in front of him. He could make it. He got closer. Nope. No, he couldn't.

He squeezed his eyes shut as he slid through the tiny space left between the moving gate and the wall. His leg scraped across the brick as he flew through.

Adrenaline flushed through him as he realized he was still alive. He shouted into the wind. Victory! Except, he didn't know what he'd scored against. Who the fuck cared, though?

He gunned it down the road in pursuit of Casey's car. Fuck the speed limit.

The minivan turned off into the courtyard of a Hertz rental company storefront. He was insanely curious about what was going on, but he kept his eyes on the prize. Something had chased Casey off Nellis Air Force Base, and he was determined to find out what. Too much crazy shit was going on for him not to run down a lead—and frankly, Casey had been his only lead.

He slowed down as he approached her car, holding back in case...well, he wasn't sure what. He was 75 percent sure that she was in some kind of trouble. He just hoped she wasn't responsible in some way for the TGO shit show they'd made of Red Flag. Because if she was, however hot he'd been for her when they'd been deployed, he was taking her down.

They were getting fairly close to downtown Vegas when she stopped off at a La Quinta hotel. He waited in a parking space near the entrance of the lot, popping his stand after about five minutes.

Casey sat in the front seat of her car, staring through the windshield at nothing. He took a breath. Maybe she'd just stood him up. Or forgotten they were supposed to be meeting? If so, that kind of made him a stalker. He took a breath, then another, waiting for some level of calm.

He didn't find it.

He hated this. Since a promotion took him out of the field

and into an office, his gut instinct hadn't been as honed as it was day in, day out, when he was an operator. People say that you never forget, but it was a lie. He didn't know if this unease he felt was real, or as fake as the flashbacks and night-mares he used to have.

He fisted his hands and straightened his fingers several times to encourage his adrenaline-spiked blood flow to pump around his extremities. Another car pulled into the parking lot and came to a stop behind Casey's car. A man in a bright red baseball hat jumped out after engaging his emergency lights, and ran into the hotel lobby, as if he were picking someone up.

This was crazy. Duke was seeing nefarious plots and con-spiracies and danger where there were none.

A small truck belonging to a local electrician pulled in and stopped at the back of the hotel, engine still running.

Duke started the engine again and was about to kick up the stand, when the man with the red baseball hat ran out of the rear emergency exit of the hotel and jumped in the elec-trician's truck. Its tires squealed and spun, as if it were going to a five-bell fire.

A panel van pulled into the parking lot and headed straight for Casey's car. Nut uh. This wasn't looking good. She'd been deliberately blocked in. It was a textbook CIA maneuver.

He turned off the engine once again, dismounted, and pulled off his helmet as he walked casually over to where she was parked. He held his iPhone to his ear, as if he were hav-ing a conversation. He laughed to his imaginary caller as the side door to the panel van opened, and two men wearing balaclava masks jumped out.

Duke started to run. He rearranged his hold on his helmet, and wrapped the strap around his hand. He watched dumbfounded as one of the men took a crowbar and smashed the driver-side window of Casey's car as she was sitting there.

Heat pulsed from his lower back, and his heart raced for a second, and then calmed as he approached the two men.

By the time Duke got close, one had cut through her seat belt and had yanked her out of the car through the window. She fought against the man, wriggling and trying to headbutt him, but he held her head against him as he tried to wrestle her into the open door of the van.

Casey wedged her feet against the van so that he couldn't put her in. *Good girl.*

Duke swung his helmet around in a circle as he reached them, and whacked the man holding Casey in the head with it. He heard a crack, and the man crumpled. Casey dropped to the ground on top of him. She scrambled up. "What the...?" she panted, panic in her eyes.

The second man was at the other side of the car, leaning in, trying to get at something in there. When he saw his buddy go down, he leapt out and jumped across the hood to get to Duke.

"Run!" Duke said to Casey as the second man raised his fist. His peripheral vision told him that she hadn't listened.

He easily ducked the man's swing and with one punch,

decked him. He frowned and shook his hand out to ease the pain.

He turned to Casey, who was backing away from him. "What are you doing? We have to get away from here."

"What are you doing here? Did you follow me? Who let you out of the base?" she asked, keeping the car between them. Suspicion etched her face.

His brain didn't compute such a drastic turn of events. "I just *saved* you, dude," he said in disbelief. "Who are they?"

She remained silent, her gaze flitting between him and her handbag, which was still on the backseat of her car. "You can get your bag, I don't care," he said, trying to keep the annoyance out of his voice. Something had spooked her. He just couldn't imagine that it was him.

He took out his iPhone again, and selected the camera function. He snapped a photo of her. "Just so I can show it to you later and remind you how ungrateful you are," he said, before bending down to pull the mask off the guy he'd clocked with his helmet. He took a photo of his face. He checked the image was in focus, but before he could stand upright, someone jumped on his back. His phone fell from his hand and skittered across the tarmacked parking lot, and under the black panel van.

*Fuck.*

The guy stuck like fucking glue to his back, strangling Duke with his arms wrapped around his neck, and his legs wrapped around his waist.

Duke took a step back and slammed the guy into the corner of the open door. He grunted, but didn't let go. Jesus. He reckoned he had about twenty seconds before he passed out, and left Casey alone with them.

Then something glanced off his head and he staggered, fighting the blackness that was threatening to overcome him. But the weight fell from his back and he propped himself up against Casey's car, trying to keep everyone in his sight.

Both men were down, and Casey was panting with excursion, or panic, with his bike helmet clutched to her chest. He straightened, knowing they didn't have a lot of time. The damn panel van had blocked the fight from the hotel's closed-circuit camera, so help wasn't coming.

He took a breath, and searched for something "I told you so"-ish that he could use to break the obvious panic Casey was in, when a second panel van came squealing into the parking lot. Shit. "Get in!" He grabbed the driver-side door of her car and squeezed into the seat, taking a valuable second to move the seat back.

"We're blocked in," Casey breathed.

"Not in a second we won't be," he replied, slamming the car into reverse and stepping hard on the gas. He spun the wheel as Casey's car made contact with the one blocking them in, moving it enough for them to get out.

He put the car into drive and sped around the side of the hotel away from the van that had stopped obviously to check that the masked men weren't dead. "Dammit. I didn't get my cell phone."

Casey looked at him as if he were crazy, but he'd opened the secure network when he'd activated the camera. Now if someone picked it up, they'd have access to his email, and all his contacts and some classified files. He punched the steering wheel. There was no telling what they'd be able to do with that.

"You want to tell me who that was, and why they tried to kidnap you?" he asked.

"It's a long story," she replied, looking out of the side window.

Anger flushed his face. "Okay. Fair enough. We'll just go back to base and see if anyone there can sort it out," he said between gritted teeth.

She grabbed his arm. "No! No, we can't go back." She took a deep breath. "I'm pretty sure those people were from TGO."

Duke was silent. And surprised at how unsurprised he was to hear it. He knew her company was sketchy. Maybe Casey could help him prove it. Get them the fuck off his base so he could order the air force pararescuers to rescue the two missing pilots. "We need to talk."

Casey was making herself crazy with unanswered questions, suspicions, and a deeply held feeling that she couldn't trust anyone except herself to get her out of this fucking mess. And she wasn't sure she could get out of this mess by herself.

She still couldn't believe that Duke Cameron had appeared out of freaking nowhere and saved her from a very definite attempt to kidnap her, or worse.

She'd brought this on herself. She'd asked the CEO of her company, Danvers, to step in and sponsor that year's Red Flag. The U.S. military had planned to cancel the event because of budget cuts. Casey remembered the euphoria she'd felt when Danvers had agreed. She'd only been with the company a matter of months, and he'd made her feel like a valuable member of the leadership team. He'd okayed her spending tens of millions of dollars. She'd never imagined she would feel that kind of a rush working in the corporate world.

Behind the throttle of an aircraft—yes, every time. But she'd long since accepted the fact that the sort of adrenaline she was used to was over. Until TGO. Until the CEO listened to her every word and included her in top-level meetings, and spent millions of dollars on her say-so. It had been an incredible rush. A different kind of rush, okay—but a rush nonetheless.

But now, at the end of the day, she was responsible for the loss of the two planes and presumably their pilots too. She'd give anything and everything to be able to dial the clock back just forty-eight hours.

"Tell me what this is all about. I know there's something off about your company. Practically everyone on base can sense it. We just can't"—Cameron sounded frustrated—"touch it. Tell me what you know." Cameron's voice was fairly calm, all things considered. As if he hadn't just beaten up two men and rescued her. Well, she'd rescued herself at the end, and that knowledge gave her a string of confidence to hold on to.

"Thank you for...helping me." She turned in her seat so she could watch his face. "Why were you following me? Or did you already know I'd be there?"

She suddenly remembered her first thought when she'd

seen him in the parking lot. That terrible thought that this was one big setup. Cameron was being paid by TGO to see if she could be trusted to keep her mouth shut. Or if she should be killed. A chill rushed through her, but she tried to keep calm and fixed her gaze on his face. Adrenaline was making it difficult to think rationally. She closed her eyes and tried to stop the panic, and fight-or-flight impulse, taking over. It had been a while since she'd had to do that. A long while. Not since she'd had to figure out takeoff vectors while under automatic weapon fire.

"I was at the officers' club. Remember? We had a date. When you cruised past at ten of, I followed you. I'd just pulled in on my bike. Damn! My bike." He turned around briefly, as if he could see it behind them. "They're going to know it was me. The only motorbike in the lot, and I"—he glanced at her—"*we* used my helmet used as a weapon. I'd be surprised if they haven't put that together already."

She breathed a little easier. Of course. Of course he wouldn't be working with TGO. What the fuck was wrong with her? But when the company she loved and trusted had suddenly tried to physically harm her, she would forgive herself for being short on trust.

"You think that's bad? I only took out third-party insurance on the rental car. Hertz is going to have me on the hook for a new freaking car."

"I'm not sure you're totally processing what just happened to you back there," Cameron said. "If you're sure it was TGO, your own company wants you for something. Or at least wants you gone somewhere. I don't really know what just happened, but I know enough to survive, evade, resist, and escape. And so do you. We did just fine."

She found herself nodding. S.E.R.E. As a military pilot, she'd been through the training. She sat straighter in her seat. With Cameron's help, she'd fulfilled her duty. To the military at least.

It was time to pick a side.

Cameron seemed to read her mind. "What are you going to do, cupcake?" he asked.

She had no answer. There was a world of things to figure out, but with the adrenaline and fear coursing through her, her brain wasn't able to work out the details she needed from it. "I just don't know. But I can't go back to base." She looked at the road stretching ahead of them into dusk. She had to hide somewhere until she figured shit out. "Maybe a hotel?"

"Are you asking me to take you to a hotel?" His voice had a swagger in it that seemed uncharacteristic for a colonel. "We were supposed to have a date first. I mean, that's the way you wuss MJ pilots like it right?"

Her mouth hung open. Then she rallied. "Fuck off, flyboy. And keep your eyes on the road. You've done enough damage already."

He grinned, and she relaxed just a tiny bit. She wondered if he'd insist on returning to Nellis, or if he'd consider sticking around. But she couldn't ask him to. She couldn't put him in the crosshairs of TGO as well. This was all on her, and if there was a fall to take, she was going to have to take it alone.

# CHAPTER 3

Chris Grove could feel the end was near. He was the chief of security at TGO, and there were far too many loose ends for his comfort. Having to wait for Mr. Danvers to give him a kill order was just creating more loose ends, rather than fewer. He never thought the day would come, but Danvers might be losing his edge.

He'd pulled into the parking lot as his men were getting up off the ground. Casey Jacobs was not subdued in the black panel van, and they had stolen no decent intel. So basically his team had failed on all the important fronts. He was furious, even more so that he couldn't just fucking kill them here and dump their bodies somewhere.

He'd kicked one of his men who was groaning on the ground, before helping him up and growling, "What the hell happened here? I sent two of you to pick up a hundred-and-ten-pound woman, and you're both here, and she isn't. Anyone care to explain?"

David Gunn's eyes were bloodshot and glazed. Gunn was one of his longest-serving security personnel. Ex-army, and usually reliable. Except today, of course. One of his pupils was dilated, and seeing Gunn's weakness just infuriated Grove more. He flexed his hands, trying not give into the urge to beat him senseless.

"There was a man with her. Some dude on a motorbike."

Grove's gaze took in the bike parked next to the entrance. Then he crouched to look at the helmet leaning against the Suburban. So, Casey had a champion? Some random biker dude had stepped in to help her? If so, he'd taken off with her, so he must have known her. So probably not a random guy off the street.

Just as he was getting up, something glinted in the parking lot lights, which had just flickered on. A phone. He stared at it for a good long time, before picking it up. "Yours?" he asked without looking at his colleague.

"No. The bastard tried to take a pic of me, but he dropped it when Sonny jumped him."

Grove didn't even bother looking at the unconscious man on the ground. He'd already passed his usefulness. He ran his finger over the screen of the iPhone, and the number pad popped up, waiting for the passcode. Too easy. He'd take it back to the hotel and be able to figure out the PIN from the layers of fingerprint impressions over the keypad.

Under his watchful eyes, the keypad disappeared and the screensaver popped up. It was one of those Osprey aircraft that special ops had used in Afghanistan. A thread of excitement shivered through him, with a tightening of anticipation. Please let this guy be special ops. He'd fucking show him who was fit for duty. He'd killed just as many people as those spec ops guys, and yet *he'd* been the one to be thrown out of the military. A familiar anger rose in him, but he tamped it down. No sense in reliving the past here, in front of his good-for-nothing men.

Mr. Danvers had shown him the way. He'd shown him that killing people was okay if it was for a good cause. *Sanctioned* was the word he used. In the military it was the magic word that meant you could engage with the enemy as you saw fit. Mr. Danvers had given him total authority to use his skills to further the ends of TGO. And he got a bonus every time he did. He made a bet that killing a spec ops guy would earn him enough to finish his bunker, and kit it out properly. A new world order was coming, and until the general population accepted it, he knew there would be war. He could ride it out for at least a year in a fully kitted out bunker. Too easy to kill the spec ops guy when he wasn't expecting it. Too fucking easy.

Also, depending on who this dead-man-walking was, Grove knew he could also get into the military systems through his iPhone. He turned it over in his hand and wondered how high a clearance this mystery guy had. Please let it be the very top level. Fuck. With a top secret clearance, he could probably access his own file and change his discharge papers from dishonorable to honorable. A thread of excitement pierced his annoyance at the abject failure of his men. Grove pocketed the phone and left, ignoring the injured men as if they weren't there; they were useless to him now.

Mr. Danvers had booked him a suite in a hotel away from the military base and off the Vegas strip. It was registered under a fake name, for which Danvers had produced a fake driving license and passport. Except Grove was pretty sure that they weren't actually fake. Mr. Danvers had contacts in many government departments, and Grove had provided him with dirt on nearly all of them. There was barely a department in the whole administration where they didn't have leverage.

One day, after a particularly successful government contract bid, Mr. Danvers had partaken in a very expensive bottle of brandy and had inferred to Grove that a video from a Russian hotel had basically got TGO the contract. A stupid video, starring an up-and-coming senator on the Ways and Means Committee, had won them a three-billion-dollar contract. Mr. Danvers was the smartest man in the world. Maybe *he* should be president.

When he arrived back at his suite, it was a fairly easy process to unlock the iPhone passcode of...He clicked through to the email account. *Fuck me!*

Grove sat back in his chair and swiveled, looking out over the rooftops and casinos of Vegas. So Colonel Duke Cameron, the commander of Red Flag, was helping Grove's target, Casey Jacobs. He let his brain knock around that thought for a few minutes, then shrugged. Dude was old now? What must he be? Early forties? Grove could take him with one arm behind his back.

He closed his eyes and took a breath. He felt a twitch in his pants as he thought about killing the commander. Not as big a twitch as he had when thinking about killing Casey

Jacobs, but she'd have to wait. He was prepared to take his time with her, anyway.

And then a thought struck him. His next job was to get rid of Missy Malden, the other "loose end" Danvers was pissed about. But she was in protective custody. Couldn't Colonel Duke Cameron order her release?

He sat up. Of course he could. Cameron was the fucking base commander.

Grove opened his email again. Jesus, but there was a bunch of stuff in there that was encrypted. Meaning Grove's boss would probably be interested in the content. He plugged a device into the iPhone and watched as it started to pick the decryption lock.

As that was being done, he composed a short email to the investigator in charge of Missy Malden's case. "After careful consideration…" Grove paused, anger suddenly engulfing him.

Those were the opening words to the letter that he'd been sent informing him of his dishonorable discharge from the army. "After careful consideration, the committee has unanimously agreed to separate you from the United States Army, with a less-than-honorable service designator."

Of course, when they found the bodies in Iraq, they downgraded his discharge to "dishonorable." He'd been killing the enemy for fuck's sake. He'd been doing exactly what they had told him to do. They were the enemy. Fucking civilians? They were still the enemy. Why couldn't they have seen that?

He fisted his hands to stop them from shaking. When he

thought about the fucking injustice, he could kill everyone that looked at him wrong. With his bare hands, with a garrote, with a machete. Hack, hack, hack. Grove visualized his last kill. His heart slowed as he pictured the warm blood running over his hands. His happy place. He took a breath. And another.

He continued to write. "After careful consideration, I have decided to release Major Missy Malden from protective custody. Please action my order immediately."

A wave of exhilaration rushed over him as he fully appreciated the turn of events. Things were finally going his way.

It told him he was on the side of righteousness, as usual. That Danvers was right, and that Grove had been right to trust him, to follow him. He would lay down his life for Danvers—he'd been more of a father to Grove than his biological father had been. At last, things seem to be coming together and he couldn't wait to pass on the good news.

He sent the encrypted data to Danvers via the TGO's corporate server in Moldova and headed out back to the base to kill Major Missy Malden. He put a call in to his boss's secure cell phone from the road.

"I've just ensured that Major Malden will be released from protective custody. I'm heading on base right now to finish it off," he said with a level of triumph he couldn't help.

"Good, good," Danvers replied thoughtfully. He paused for long enough that Grove checked his phone to ensure the connection was still good. "No. Stand down. I want Lieutenant Colonel Janke to do it. You run the op, but I want him to pull the trigger. Then we'll own him."

Grove's heart started racing. He was being rejected by his boss. He held his breath to prevent the sound of his heaving chest from reaching the phone.

"Now, now," Danvers said with a lulling tone. "I know you're the most capable, but I can't risk losing you. It's a dangerous hit, and after these months of taking money from us, Janke needs to put his trigger finger where his mouth is. He's talked a good game, got us a few smaller contracts, promised us things that he's delivered, but now we need him to fully integrate. So, there's no backing out. So there's absolutely no risk of him turning whistle-blower. You understand."

Grove did understand, and said as much before hanging up. He'd killed a former attempted whistle-blower. Well, made it look like suicide at least. But he wondered: Had Danvers set him up in the same way he was setting up Colonel Janke? Was that how he'd brought him into TGO? And did he really care what brought him to TGO, and Danvers?

He'd think about it when it was a little quieter. Once he'd got rid of Missy Malden *and* Casey Jacobs. He put a credit card watch on Casey and figured he'd let them get a little farther away from Vegas before pulling the trigger. Maybe.

# CHAPTER 4

Do you have anywhere to go? Parents, a sister, somewhere you can lay low?"

She couldn't help but notice that he said "you" rather than "we." Her heart sank a little. But she couldn't blame him. He had a military base to run, two pilots to find, and a multinational training exercise to manage.

"Not really." She turned her head toward the darkness outside the car. She watched the signposts as they flashed by. What had happened to her? In the space of two days her whole world had crumbled. She had elderly parents in Florida, but she wasn't about to put them in the crosshairs of this shit show.

"How much cash do you have on you?" he asked.

She had no idea. She pulled her purse from the rear seat to the front and groped inside for her wallet. "A twenty."

Cameron looked in his rearview mirror, used his directional, swung a 180-degree turn across two lanes of thankfully empty roads, and gunned the throttle back toward Vegas.

"What are you doing? I can't go back!" Fear trickled through her again, and she clasped her purse to her as if she were an old lady on a bus.

"It's all right. Trust me," he said, reluctantly, as if he wasn't used to explaining his actions to anyone—which come to think of it, he probably wasn't.

But that wasn't going to cut it with her. She still wasn't sure exactly whom to trust. "This is my life that's in danger—not yours. Tell me where we're going."

"We're going back to Vegas, we're going to withdraw as much cash as we can downtown. Then we're going to leave the car somewhere. I'll pick up a new car at the airport, and we'll stay the night in a hotel."

That didn't sound like a good idea at all. "No. We have to get as far away from here as possible." The farther she got from Nellis, and her company, and its employees, the safer she'd feel.

He sighed, as if she were an impossibly stupid child. "That's what they'll expect us to do. Always assess your enemy, and confound them with your actions. They'll clearly expect us to run—that's what they were trying to prevent you from doing presumably—ergo, we stay in Vegas for a little bit. Maybe in the hotel closest to the one where they tried to lift you. They would absolutely never look there."

Casey's stomach churned at the thought of going back toward danger. Vegas had definitely lost its luster for her. But when she analyzed her thought process—as they'd been taught to do as pilots—she realized that running away from trouble wasn't going to stop TGO from chasing her. Wasn't going to make her job miraculously unchanged. Wasn't going to make this rental car pristine again. She may as well face what was coming head-on, and just hope that she could rely on Cameron to help her.

"Okay, but don't blame me when we both get put in jail for fifty years," she said.

"Just what the fuck did you do?" he asked. "Because if I find out you had anything to do with the crash, and the loss of those two pilots, I will put you in jail myself." He didn't sound as if he was joking, that was for sure.

"I swear I didn't." She stopped short of saying what she desperately wanted to. That she was sure her company had installed illegal software onto both planes. That if she told anyone she ran the risk of being ruined and—her thoughts flickered to James Turner, the attempted whistle-blower—maybe even killed. Could her company really be that ruthless? She needed to figure out what her next move should be, but in order to do that, she needed to know what her company was actually capable of.

"What is all this about then? Your own company tries to abduct you, and you're not even curious why? You didn't call the police…Actually, why didn't you call the police?"

Her mouth fell open. "Really? You expect me to go to the Vegas police and tell them I just busted out of a locked-down base, that security tried to stop me, gave chase, and tried to take me back? I'm pretty sure the police will just hand me over to them."

"Who was in the minivan that left just ahead of you? Was that something to do with you too?" he asked, jumping from one subject to another like the well-trained interrogator that he probably was.

She could tell him that. "That was the Animal and friends. They were tired of sitting on their asses and leaving the rescue to TGO. They asked me to bust them out so that they could do their own search and rescue."

"And you just let them?" Disbelief echoed in the car.

She shrugged. "I owed him."

Cameron huffed an unbelieving laugh. "What could you possibly owe *him*?"

She sat up straighter. "What do you mean '*him*'? Like he's the last person on earth who could have done something for me in the past?"

"Well, isn't he? He's a show pony. All that hoisting himself out of the cockpit like he was a gymnast on the rings or something."

The smug bastard. How dare he? "Careful," she said, dabbing at her face as if showing him where crumbs were on his. "You've got a bit of jealousy here."

He snorted.

"Have you honestly never flown with him downrange?" she asked.

"Why would I? He's conventional warfare, and I'm—"

"—anything other than conventional." She nodded. It was true. Spec ops really did think they were flighting a different war sometimes. "I flew with him a lot. And he saved my crew, me and my aircraft on more than one occasion. That's why

I gave him a pass. That's why I'll always give him a pass. He took out a surface-to-air missile nest, and then the missile they let off at me seconds before they blew up. He was laughing over the radio as he did it. It was locked onto us. We had limited maneuverability. My crew had already pretty much said our goodbyes to each other."

She paused, tears welling up in her eyes as she remembered why they'd been there and were so vulnerable. They were one engine down and were searching for an air-refueler so they could…

Nope. She wasn't going there. She sniffed and glared out the window, widening her eyes so the air would dry the unshed tears.

She grabbed a tissue from her bag and swiped at her nose. "And by the way, the reason he looks like a gymnast, is because he was a gymnast. An Olympic medalist. You know how many South Koreans joined the military after he did?" She didn't wait for his answer. "Over three thousand. He knows what's important, and he knows how to motivate the people he works with." She paused. "If you had a way to get people out of the base to look for the pilots, wouldn't you have taken it? You wouldn't have thought it more important to have as many eyes out there as possible? You would have let him out?"

She looked into the darkness, before turning back. "And, by the way. He never mentioned that he saved our lives—ever—until this evening, when he called in his favor to go rescue pilots who aren't even Korean. So, don't talk to me about him like that, okay?"

\* \* \*

Cameron's hands tightened around the steering wheel as he remembered the mission she was talking about. He remembered feeling impotent as he listened to the ground troops on the radio. They'd been utterly surrounded, with the nearest backup too far away to do any good. Cameron had known the unit of ground troops was going to die, everyone in the control room had. Until Major Casey Jacobs's voice had come over the radio. "This is Double Down. I've got ordnance, and I'm five minutes out."

He'd celebrated inwardly. Until another airman in the room half-whispered, "They can get to them, but they won't be able to get back. They're out of fuel. And whatever ordnance they have, they'll have to shove off the ramp."

Everyone had known what that meant. She'd have to descend to an altitude that would eat up her remaining fuel, and make her an easy target.

"Hey! I'm talking to you!" Casey punched him in the arm, bringing him right back to the present.

"Stop hitting me," he ground out, embarrassed that he'd slipped so easily into his own thoughts.

"Pay attention to me then. You can't insult my friends and then just tune out when I'm explaining things to you." She folded her arms.

*What?* "I'm sorry? I rescue you from armed thugs, help you escape, have you tell me abso-fucking-lutely nothing about what you're involved in, and I'm supposed to be listening to every word you say? I'll fucking listen to you when you tell me what is going on, and what happened to my pilots.

I don't even know if you're legit. Maybe you did something that caused those aircraft to crash? What is it you actually do for TGO?"

He had no idea why that just exploded out of him. He didn't really think she had anything to do with it, did he? Maybe he did. Maybe subconsciously, that's exactly what he thought. He wracked his brain for reasons. For method. What could she gain by pretending to be attacked by her own company? To gain his trust? But why?

"I don't think—"

"Zip it," he growled. He needed to think this through. But his brain kept stuttering on what he knew about Casey. What he knew about the Animal, well, what he'd thought he'd known about the Animal.

*What he thought he knew about Casey.*

In truth, he knew nothing about her beyond what was in her records. So she'd risked her life for others a bunch of times. They'd all done that. That was what they'd all signed up for. He knew about her work record, and the way he'd fantasized about her while they were both downrange. Not that he'd ever given her the impression that he wanted her. He'd come real close once when they both dived for the same bunker to avoid incoming mortar fire. She'd made a sexy groan when she'd thrown herself into the trench. It had sparked an uncomfortable twenty minutes when they'd been so close he had felt the soft warmth of her breath on the side of his face. Was that it? Was his dick doing the thinking now? The trusting? The crazy desire he had to reach out and stroke her face, her hair...*dammit.*

He was beginning to wish he hadn't asked her out that evening. But then presumably she'd either be dead, or forcibly returned to the TGO fold. Fuck.

He had to get his head into gear and make a decision. Deliver her to the police, or back to base, and let the investigation team get to the bottom of TGO, and Casey herself if necessary. Or take to the road and help her figure out this shit show she'd got herself into. And bring TGO down, by hook or by fucking crook. And as far as he was concerned, the company was full of crooks. He just wondered if Casey was one of them.

The former was the responsible officer-in-charge decision. He was the commander of Red Flag, and even being away from base in the middle of this crisis was making him nervous. The latter was the irresponsible option, the lone-wolf, the wildfire option, guaranteed to get him fired, or worse.

Visions of his fishing charter operation in Florida—his retirement dream—faded to black. There was no choice really. His heart rate steadied, he set his mind on the op, not on the woman sitting beside him. Except, that was an impossibility. His head was overwhelmed with her smell, that crazy red dress she was wearing, the impossibly high sandals.

At the next rest stop, such as it was, they both maxed out their cards at the sketchiest-looking ATM he'd ever seen. At least if someone was skimming numbers from the machine, there wasn't a penny more that they could get out of their accounts.

"I'm so fucked. I owe Hertz a car, I have no job," Casey

grumbled as she took the last of their withdrawals from the machine.

"You've forgotten that your company may also be trying to kill you," he replied drily.

She glared at him. "Thanks. I hadn't forgotten. It just sounded unbelievable in my head. You know, until you just said that. Now that's all I'll be thinking about."

"Nope. But hey, don't worry, if you don't tell me what you know, and they kill you anyway, they'll have won," he said, shrugging, hoping that he could push her to reveal what she knew.

She stared at him, a long gaze that unnerved him. Her eyes fluttered down to the ground, and then back up to his face. She frowned, a look of fear in her eyes. He wished he could take that back. Wished he could just take her in his arms and…fuck, he didn't know. Take her to a movie? Something normal. Something that didn't involve being a target.

She bit her lip, and looked at the cash she'd just withdrawn, as if she didn't recognize it.

"Casey. You all right?"

She looked up at him again, then down at her money. She sighed and tucked in into her purse. "You can be a real douche, you know that?" Her tone was mild. Exhausted even.

"Yeah. I know that." He held out his hand to her.

After a few seconds she placed her hand in his. As they walked back to the car, he kept an eye on the people who passed them, the cars entering the rest area, and ensured the ones around their car had been there when they got out.

But while his brain was processing the information, something else in him was reveling in the fact that he was actually touching Casey Jacobs. Her hand was in his.

He watched as she got into the car. As she disappeared from view, he steeled himself against the emotion that was threatening his focus. Because whether she knew it or not, they were on a mission now. And nothing stood between him and a successful mission. He glanced at Casey. No, not even her.

# CHAPTER 5

Casey was trying not to let her utter and total desire for Cameron show. She crossed her legs against the ache between them and tapped her foot as if she were casually listening to music.

As soon as he'd held his hand out for hers, everything skittered out of her mind, except him. Except the memories of seeing him downrange, and wanting him way back then. She admitted to herself that she'd suffered from a little bit of hero worship back then. He'd been a special ops pilot, in the seat of a CV-22 Osprey—the aircraft that could take off like a helicopter, and then fly like a plane. It meant more often than not, he got in the fight too. It could land and take off from anywhere, dropping air commandos out of the back door, or letting them fast-rope.

More than once she'd seen him bring in a mortally wounded aircraft full of men, in a way that no other pilot could do. He'd get out of the smoldering plane, covered in oil, and the troops he'd been carrying would all but kiss him on the mouth they were so grateful.

She never saw him at any of the movie evenings on base, or any of the socials. The only time she they crossed paths was at briefings, and in the chow hall. And a couple of times she'd refueled him midair with her aircraft. She'd relished those times that he'd talked to her through her headset. It had always sounded like he was right next to her, talking directly into her ear.

And that one time they'd found themselves taking cover from incoming firepower. They'd spent maybe ten minutes so close to each other that she could have kissed him without moving. It had been the longest ten minutes of her life. She'd fantasized about seducing him right there. But instead she'd just tried to regulate her breathing, worried about the onions she'd had in her salad that lunchtime, and then accepted his hand to climb out of the bunker, with a brief "thanks" before returning to her crib.

When he'd asked her out earlier that day, she'd been thrilled, and distraught. She was pretty sure he'd only done it to pump her for information…but on the other hand, when he was ranting at her earlier, she was pretty sure he'd called her out for ditching him on their date. He'd called it a date.

They said nothing in the car until he pulled off at a motel about two blocks behind the hotel parking lot she'd been attacked in. The illuminated sign blinked: OT L.

"Really?" she muttered, looking at the peeling paint and the one room door that seemed to have a large stain on the bottom half. From the parking lot, it looked like blood.

"You want a nicer hotel? One that will insist on credit cards and IDs?" he asked testily.

"Nope." She got out and looked around. The rooms formed a double-story U shape around a parking lot and an empty swimming pool that had grass growing out the cracks in its sides.

Old crime scene police tape fluttered across the parking lot as they got out. She caught Cameron's eye, and he suppressed a grin. "We'll go check in, and then I'll move the car back to the scene of the crime." He took in the crime scene tape again. "You know, the other crime."

"Okay, but what if they find it?" she asked.

"Actually, that's a good point. I'm going to leave the keys in the car, and hopefully someone will steal it. At least if they're tracking, or trying to trace, the rental, then they'll be chasing their tails for a while."

"But we would be carless," she repeated as if talking to a child.

He grinned. "I'm never carless. The U.S. government gave me lessons in not being carless."

She rolled her eyes and shrugged. Of course the military would have taught him how to steal cars.

She looked back at the motel. If it had been just a tad cleaner, she may have been excited about spending the night in the hotel with Cameron, but frankly, she was pretty sure she'd be scared to touch anything in the room. Not to mention worried that they'd be sharing their rooms with other, smaller occupants.

They opened the creaky door to the musty office. It was

dark, except for a television flickering light behind the desk. A scruffy man, about twenty-three, quickly jumped up and started pressing buttons on the remote. Not fast enough for her to miss what he'd been watching. Free porn in the hotel she guessed. His frantic button pushing had landed on CNN.

She let Cameron do the talking as her eyes wandered around the office. Faded photos of Hollywood actors and actresses were pinned on the wall, as if they had once stayed in there.

Her attention snapped back to the man when he said, "Seven-fifty an hour, or twenty-nine ninety-nine for the whole night. Before she could laugh, Cameron slapped a fifty on the counter and pulled Casey close to him with his arm around her neck.

"The change is yours if you don't disturb us," he said, before roughly yanking her face to his. His lips landed hard on hers, and he opened her mouth under his. His hands ran down her back and then pulled her pelvis hard against his.

Casey was so startled that her eyes flew open, despite the heat that ran through her, taking her from disgust at her surroundings to hopeless needing in no time at all. Wetness pooled between her legs, and her consciousness fought the surrender his mouth was forcing upon her. His hand went to her breast, cupping the outside and dragging his thumb over the top edge of her bra. Her eyes closed again. And then she remembered that they had an audience. Was that Cameron's thing? She was about to step back when the clerk spoke.

"Get a room," he muttered, clanking a key against the desk.

She tried to move away from Cameron, but he held her close, pressing her face into his shoulder, squishing her nose so firmly that she could barely breathe.

"Thanks, sport," he said as he all but dragged her out of the office.

"What was that?" Casey asked, trying hard to find some indignation in her voice.

"We were on CNN. Shit. We have to get to the room," he said, looking at the number on the key. "Thirteen."

*Of course.* "What do you mean we were on CNN?" she asked, fear crushing the desire she'd been relishing a scant few seconds earlier.

"CNN had photos of us on the news. And it did not look like Don Lemon was going to give us an award for anything. I didn't want the clerk to look at the TV and recognize us, so I had to get him to remember something else when he thought about us. Not our faces."

"Yeah, I suspect he'll be thinking about you groping my breasts. So good job," she said trying to hold on to just one of the many emotions vying for prominence. Fear, need, and now embarrassment that for a few seconds, she'd thought that he wanted her so much, that he couldn't wait until they were alone.

Cameron led her up the outside stairs to the second floor. Thirteen was a corner room, with a view over the almost empty parking lot.

As soon as they got in, he grabbed the remote and clicked the TV on. She sniffed the stale smoky air and nearly gagged.

Immediately an image of a man going down on a woman

on a pool table filled the screen. Her moans were very, very loud. Despite her anxiety, Casey's mouth twitched, trying to hold back a laugh. Men were total suckers for the loud fake moans.

Cameron didn't even really seem to notice. He found CNN after going through several channels, but by the time the familiar logo and ticker tape clicked on, they were already talking about something the vice president had said earlier that day. He pressed another button, just as the news footage showed the vice president on a White House podium saying, "We have absolute confidence in TechGen-One's ability—"

Cameron flipped the channel before either of them registered what he'd said.

"Wait, go back," she said, but he was already on it.

Don Lemon was back on the screen. "…so I imagine that has put TGO's shareholders at ease. The vice president has firmly endorsed military contractor TGO in the face of suspicions over the crash of two aircraft during a training exercise at Nellis Air Force Base. Earlier, a White House spokesperson said that they were receiving regular updates from TGO about the air crash investigation. So the question remains, where is Nellis Air Force Base commander, Colonel Duke Cameron, and TGO employee Casey Jacobs? They've been missing since the crash, and TGO spokesperson has declared them persons of interest in the investigation. This just a few days before TGO signs a thirty-billion-dollar, ten-year deal to supply NATO military forces with their state-of-the-art technologies. This is a breaking story, and we'll bring you more when we get it. Stay tuned to find out why your children's playground may be lethal. A full report, after these messages."

Casey sank onto the foot of the bed. "Sweet baby Jesus. What just happened?"

"God-damn-it!" he said, and then paused. "Playgrounds are lethal now?"

She gaped at him, and he shrugged. "Worth a try. Thought it might distract you from your unplanned notoriety. Did it work?"

"Not really, no. What do we do now?" she asked.

"The good news is that the dude downstairs is probably already whacking off again, so he won't remember us for a while—assuming he ever tunes into a news program, that is. I'm going to move the car, but when I come back, all your cards better be on the table. I need to know everything you know about TGO, the crash, and why they were trying to lift you earlier. Everything. If I think you've left anything out, I'm going to drop you so fast..." He stared at her for a moment, and left the room, closing the door very quietly.

Casey stared at the door for a long time after he left. She couldn't tell him everything. She just couldn't. Right now she had a target on her back because of the panicked phone call she'd made to head office. But she was damned if she was going to paint a target on Cameron's back too.

She slumped as she stared at the TV screen. Yup. The anchor was explaining how deadly playgrounds could be. Casey closed her eyes and took a deep breath.

The room was too hot, but when she touched the thermostat, something sticky transferred to her fingers. She shuddered, and took a good look around the room. It was painted yellow…actually, it seemed to have been painted white, but the upper parts of the walls were stained in yellow, which accounted for the strong smell of smoke.

The bed had a coin slot attached, which she assumed from the movies and TV she'd watched, made the bed vibrate, although the instructions had worn off.

She was too worried to look closely at the bed, in case she actually had to lie down on it to sleep. She felt a lot more comfortable opting for the rickety chair against the wall by the door. Oh shit. Was that chair there because the lock on the door didn't work?

She tried locking it. Nope. It didn't work. She shoved the chair under the door handle, and then tried opening it. It held. Well kudos to jack-off guy for at least "trying" to secure the rooms.

She looked into the bathroom at the back of the room. It wasn't too bad. White cracked tile on the floor, walls, and ceilings, and the U-bend of the toilet was brown. Lovely. The shower had no curtain or anything to prevent the whole room getting wet, but the floor did have a drain, right in the middle. Only hand towels though.

Great—she had only the clothes she was in—a dress, panties and bra, and a pair of sneakers in the car…she turned to the door, as if she could ask Cameron to bring them in before he abandoned the car. Shit. She was stuck with her strappy sandals. She turned back to the bathroom. There was no comfortable way she could shower either. Her day was just getting better and better.

She understood that she was trying to distract herself from the mess she was in. She was wanted by the police, her company was accusing her of something she didn't do, and it seemed to also have the ear of the White House. Suddenly she wished she could go back just a few hours to when her main worry was about breaching the confidentiality clause on her contract.

But at least she wasn't alone. At least Cameron was there with her. She hoped. She fretted about what she could tell him. How she could give him enough information that he wouldn't dump her. But without telling him enough that may get him killed too. Or ruined.

Suddenly the door rattled. She jumped. "Who is it?"

"The fucking tooth fairy," Cameron growled.

She took the chair away from the door, and it burst open. He clocked her holding the chair. "What are you doing?"

"It's the only way to lock the door," she said, shutting the door and shoving the chair under the handle.

He shook his head and dropped a couple of Target shopping bags.

"A gift? For me? You shouldn't have," she said, sitting on the bed and opening the bags.

There were two towels, two toothbrushes, some toothpaste, soap, and a five-pack of Fruit of the Loom cotton underwear. "I was wrong. You totally should have. Thank you. I'd been eyeing up the chair to sleep on. I haven't wanted to look at the bed too closely. Now I can sleep on the towel tonight and shower in the morning." She closed her eyes at the relief of being able to lie down to sleep. Not that she hadn't slept in her fair share of awkward places, but since leaving the military, she'd been pretty spoiled.

Then he put both hands behind his back and pulled out the sneakers she thought had been history. "Your feet are tiny. They fit in my back pocket." He held them out to her, but as she stretched to grab them, he pulled them out of her reach. "You're not getting anything until you tell me what's going on. What do you know about the crash? What do you know about TGO's involvement in it? And why are they telling the national media that we had something to do with it?"

He dragged the chair across the floor and sat astride it, resting his arms on the back. He could tell she was itching to get up, but he shifted the chair close enough that she couldn't move away without actually asking him to move. She crossed her legs and leaned back slightly.

"Look, I really want to tell you everything, but I just can't," she began.

"Okay, no problem. The room's yours until tomorrow—I'm headed back to base." He made a production of getting up, but he hadn't even gone as far as lifting his ass of the seat when she protested.

"Let me start at the beginning. It's not like we have anything better to do right now," she said.

He raised an eyebrow. He had plenty of better things to do, but to his consternation, all he could think about was unwrapping the ties on her dress. Jesus, they were alone in a hotel room. How were they not already naked?

She held up a hand in protest. "Okay, I know you have better things to do…"

The side of his mouth twitched. He had a nasty suspicion he would start getting hard if he thought any more about getting Casey naked. Jesus. This was going to be a long night.

"…when I signed it—" she was saying.

"Wait, what? Sorry, go back to the beginning. I was thinking about…something else."

She raised her eyebrows. "I thought you wanted to hear this? What in the world were you thinking about?"

"I'll tell you later."

"Oka-ay," she dragged it out as if he were a child. "Last year I left the military. There wasn't really a good career path for an MJ-130J pilot, except as an airline pilot, so when TGO approached me to consult on their pilot programs…" Her voice trailed off, as her eyes flickered to her left. He let her absorb what she was thinking.

"And?"

Her eyes met his again. "I was flattered. But you know how we all felt about military contractors. Urgh, God, I can still see them driving around the Iraqi compound in their stupid ultraconspicuous four-wheel drives, with Ray-Bans on, and stupid music blaring. You know—living the dream, earning ten times as much as we were, with none of the responsibility or rules."

He nodded. "And suddenly that seemed like a good idea to you?" he asked, wondering just how hard she'd sold out.

"No! No. Danvers wasn't like that." She paused. "He seemed different. Totally supportive of the military. Willing to shell out for anything people asked for. He was generous to a fault. He supplied every firebase in Afghanistan with radio and video game equipment, just because someone tweeted about how isolated they felt. He did it for free. Didn't tell anyone. I only knew because he had me get the Army Post Office address for the firebase. He was the real deal. I thought."

Her eyes pleaded with him to understand. And he kind of did. But he wasn't letting her off that easy. "What happened?"

"That's just it—nothing happened. I'm on my old unit's Facebook page, and they announced that it was likely that Red Flag would be canceled for budgetary reasons. I didn't think too much about it until the next board meeting, where Danvers said he was looking for sponsorship opportunities. Demanded everyone think outside the box. There was dead silence in the boardroom, so I suggested funding Red Flag…" She looked down, and seemed to regroup. "I didn't actually expect him to agree, I was just trying to demonstrate that I could think 'outside the box.'"

He felt an unnatural urge to comfort her. "So you tried to impress your boss. I'm pretty sure that's what everyone does."

Suddenly she seemed ticked off. "Yes, but my ridiculous need for approval may have gotten people killed."

"*May have* being the operative words there." He gave her a second. "Then what?"

"Then what, what? We came here, there was an accident, and—"

"And people from your company tried to kidnap you? Just

Vegas high jinks?" He injected an incredulous tone into his voice so that she understood he wasn't taking any of her bull-shit answers.

She flopped back onto the bed and stared at the ceiling. He glanced up at it. There were certainly enough stains on it for a comprehensive Rorschach test, and he was pretty sure he could identify most of them as being bodily fluids and maybe exploding beer.

He kicked one of her dangling legs to get her attention. She sat back up.

"Why did the planes crash?"

"I can't tell you," she said, to his rising anger.

He opened his mouth to protest.

"You don't understand. When I joined TGO, I spent a whole day signing and initialing my contract. It was over eight hundred pages long, and it included a confidentiality clause. If I talk about the business to anyone, I lose every-thing." Her eyes dipped down. "I also heard that they may have been responsible for the death of a TGO guy who tried to accuse them of something before. In Connecticut."

For sure he knew that TGO wasn't the upstanding corpo-ration it claimed to be, but he was finding it difficult to get his head around the fact that he witnessed masked men try to take Casey, and that they had killed a whistle-blower. It sounded more like a company from 1980s Soviet Russia than a twenty-first-century American company. One that clearly had the backing of the White House. "Are you sure the men in the parking lot were TGO?" he asked.

"Dave was...yeah, I'm sure. He worked on Chris Grove's

security team. He asked me out once. He has a tattoo on his hand. I recognized it."

"And you're sure this wasn't an unrequited love thing?" He had to ask.

"Yup. He's married now. He's nice, you know? He must have been given orders. They don't work for TGO, really. Our security is a wholly owned subsidiary."

"I'm sure that makes it easier for plausible deniability," he said.

"Not plane crashes, though. They couldn't have been responsible…" She stopped talking.

"Tell me about the plane crash," he said. Now they were getting to the crux of the matter.

"I can't tell you anything. The less you know, the more protected you are," she said, laying a hand on his arm.

He looked at her hand on him and said, "That's cute. You're protecting me." He rolled his eyes. "Tell me."

"No." She met his eyes steadily.

He got up, and this time she let him. He swung the chair back to the wall by the door and patted his pockets, as if he were checking everything before he left. *Come on. Stop me.* "Okay, I'm going. I won't tell anyone where you are, but I parked your car in the Bellagio parking deck. The keys are under the driver's seat. You should move on as soon as possible. Wait until rush hour, don't be tempted to leave too early or you'll be noticeable."

"I appreciate your help. Really," she said sincerely. "I'll hope to see you…at the other side of all this." She stood up and held out her hand.

God-fucking-damn everything. She was calling his bluff, whether she knew it or not. He took her hand and shook it, planning to walk out and call Nellis for a ride back, but he didn't. Her hand was warm and dry in his. *Let it go. Let it go.* Everything in his body was telling him to stay with her. To ensure she was safe. To protect her. It killed him that she'd so believed in her new company, and that her trust had been her downfall.

"Shit." He yanked his hand from hers, turned away and ran it through his hair. "Fucking tell me, will you?"

"I won't."

*"Fuck."*

# CHAPTER 6

Cameron agreed to stay the night, just until Casey could figure out her next move. He could have left, and she wouldn't have thought any less of him; this wasn't his fight. But he elected to stay, even though she wouldn't budge on what she knew about the crash.

In fact, all she had were suspicions. But she thought she had a plan at least. She lay on the bed as if she'd been laid out for a funeral. Fully dressed, on her back, on top of the towel that Cameron had bought them. She didn't dare move in case she got some kind of yuck on her skin. She shuddered every time she thought about the cleanliness of the bed.

Cameron wasn't having that difficulty. He'd taken his shirt off, revealing a heavily tattooed torso and shoulder. Certainly some of the designs were related to his missions. There was a series of dates, but she couldn't see too much from her dead-in-a-coffin position. She'd tried to see more, but the light was dim, and she didn't want to stare. Or rather, she didn't want to be *caught* staring.

He talked in his sleep. Nothing intelligible, but he seemed to be having a conversation with someone. She'd tried to sleep, but she couldn't. She was bone-tired, but her brain was keeping her awake. Not to mention her hormones. After everything, she'd found it hard to not think about wrapping her legs around him and having her way with him. So she spent her night either thinking about the situation she was in, or thinking about having sex with Cameron, and wondering why he wasn't trying to have sex with her. In every movie she'd ever seen, they'd be doing it by now.

Needless to say, she hadn't slept a wink by the time Cameron woke. Her stomach was tight with a lack of food, too much anxiety, and too little sleep. She needed coffee, and a new set of clothes, and while she was thinking about it, how about a new identity and a new life? Not to mention a pee. At least, one thing she did have—a plan.

Cameron got up and headed straight for the bathroom without saying a word. She sat up, put on the bedside light, and grabbed the remote. She debated for a second whether or not to—she really didn't want to see her photo on the news again. Luckily, she sat through the whole "top of the hour" news and she wasn't mentioned once.

Idly she punched the remote for the different channels, and of course, she landed on a porn channel just as Cameron was coming out of the bathroom. She quickly switched it back to CNN.

"Don't let me stop you getting off. You need some privacy?" he joked.

She stared at him a little too long, filtering her brain for a decent response. Her addled brain came up with nothing.

"Okaaaay then," he said with a grin.

Casey suddenly had a weird flashback to Afghanistan. They only exchanged maybe a hundred words the entire time they were there. Occasionally saying hello, asking how one another was. And yet, a couple of years later, they were on the run and sharing a motel room.

"I know nothing about you," she said, staring at him. "I mean...last night was..." She cleared her throat. "...the most time I've ever spent with you. And here we are. Don't you think that's weird?"

"I guess so," he said with a frown. "I feel like I've known you more than that though. We didn't hang out down-range?"

"No. Maybe you're thinking about someone else?" That didn't make her feel any better.

He smiled absently. "I don't think so. You're not that easy to forget."

A tingle flashed through her, but she tamped it down, along with her whole night of longing. "In a good way? Or..."

"That's for me to know," he replied, pulling his T-shirt back on. "You can take the shower first." He nodded toward the bathroom. "Then we need to make a plan."

"I already have one. I mean, it's a plan for me," she said matter-of-factly. "I wasn't expecting you to be a part of it."

"So, convince me to."

"Convince you to what?" She was confused.

He spoke slowly, as if she were educationally challenged. "Convince me to be a part of your plan."

A brightness flashed through her, turning her heavy burden into a lighter, more hopeful one. And then she overthought it. How was he expecting her to convince him? With words about her plan, or with sex? And did she really mind either way? *God damn, girl. What's the matter with you?*

"I can tell you my plan?" she said with an embarrassingly hoarse voice.

"You better, because my plan involves…rampage and ugliness. Mostly, anyway. Yours may have more finesse."

She held an image of him plowing through crowds of bad people to help her. He was shirtless, camo makeup on his face. Yup, he was basically Rambo in her head..

"Well?" he asked, snapping her out of her reverie.

"Hmm? Oh right. The plan." She puffed air out of her cheeks. It would be the first time she'd articulated her plan, and she wanted to be sure she was thinking through all the pitfalls before blurting out something stupid.

"Just tell me already," he said, sitting on the old chair that was bracing the door shut.

"Look—before I tell you, I want to remind you that you're under no obligation to come, agree, or even have an opinion. I'm not expecting you to do anything."

"Okaaay."

"The first thing I need is Internet access, obviously from someplace where no one is going to track me down."

Cameron opened his mouth to speak, but she held up her hand to stop him. "I'm not going to log on to any of my accounts. I just need to do some basic research on the guy who tried to whistle blow on TGO. James Turner. Apparently, he was sued to the point of destitution, and then he 'committed suicide.'" She used air quotes to show that she didn't believe that he had, in fact, killed himself. "I need to see for myself what the record says, and then I want to go to Connecticut to find someone who knew him. It's been a few years—maybe someone will talk about him now. Only then will I be able to assess my own risk. And yours, if I'm being honest. I want to tell you everything, but not if it's just going to get us killed." She paused, trying to gauge his reaction, but his face was a blank.

He took a breath. And then said nothing. Should she continue with her plan? Why did she feel like she was waiting for a teacher to react to her thesis?

"Then what?" he said.

"Depending on the outcome, we go to my apartment in Alexandria, and retrieve the pr—" She stopped herself from saying project files. "—a thing from my safe that may help." There was no way she could tell him that she had all the product specs and trial reports for PreCall. She didn't think anyone knew she had them. She'd got them from the dead-records room when she first joined—ironically she'd taken them home so that she could impress the board with her product knowledge, and now having them might just save her from her company. She was sure that those trial reports showed exactly the same malfunction as the two aircraft that had crashed at Red Flag: static, overcorrecting controls, and inability for the pilot to reestablish manual control.

"Then what?"

"Then we find someone who can investigate for us. Me. For me. Sorry, I'm not assuming—"

"Jesus Christ. Just stop with the assuming and the obligating shit. I'm in. I can help with logistics. Maybe find someone at the Pentagon who will read your reports—"

She pulled a face, and he stopped talking. After a second he nodded too. "Okay, not someone at the Pentagon."

"I'm just worried that it's a big ask. I mean, we'd be asking for someone to put their career on the line for people they don't know. And if they did, would that make them a target too? I mean, these people have the vice president of the United States on their side, it seems."

Cameron nodded. "Okay, we can think about that when we know what we're dealing with."

Casey closed her eyes briefly. Calm settled over her. He was coming with her. He wasn't going to turn her in or abandon her. Then she looked back up and searched his eyes. "Thank you for believing me. Thank you for coming with me. I feel less…alone."

He nodded briefly. "We'll call it the benefit of the doubt for now."

"I'll take it."

They remained silent, and suddenly the room was too small, the morning had become way too bright for her to cope with. She jumped up to go to the bathroom.

Anything to give her a little privacy from Cameron's

steady gaze. She needed a place where she could pull every terrified face she had, every relieved sob, and not have to worry that he was judging her.

Cameron fought between maintaining his rigid exterior, and grabbing her and taking her to the shower with him. Okay, so he did believe her. He knew who she was inside, and he knew she wouldn't have done anything to put other pilots at risk. But he figured it wouldn't hurt her to think that she had to win him over.

Did that make him bad? Maybe. But nothing spoke quite as loud as the need to touch her. To kiss her. To possess her if only for a few hours. He laughed inwardly at his own words. A few hours. More like he'd only last minutes.

He took a breath of the stale air and turned to the grimy window. It was too bright outside. It looked like it was about midday, but it wasn't. They'd woken up way too early, although he wasn't sure either of them had gotten much sleep. Casey had smudges under her eyes, and he'd tried to lie so still he wouldn't disturb her, that she wouldn't feel uncomfortable sharing a bed with him. He wasn't sure if he'd slept more than forty minutes in total.

Neither of them would be in fighting form unless they found somewhere to relax. And he thought he might have an idea of where they could go. They could spend the night and get fixed up to go to Connecticut. "You want to stay and shower, or do you want to press on?"

"We should press on, I guess," she said, looking with a wince toward the bathroom. "I'll need something to wear too. I'm going to feel like I'm doing the walk of shame all day if I don't change." She actually blushed and looked away from him.

He wanted to laugh, to say something funny to diffuse her discomfort, but instead he jumped up. Action was better than words. "I'm going to go boost us a car."

"Where from?" she asked.

"Long-term parking at the airport. Find a car that's recently been parked. Take a chance that the owners won't report it stolen until they get back. Hope that it's a few days at least. Pay the lost-ticket charge. Easy as that." It was actually standard operating procedure for special operators who had been stranded anywhere hostile, and he figured that if the government had trained him to do it, then it was only semi-illegal.

"Well let's try not to ruin it. They might not have great insurance." She frowned at him.

"We'll even take it through a car wash before we leave it, if it'll make you feel better." He had no intention of washing the car, but he also had no intention of damaging it either. He just hoped that TGO had the same respect for others' property.

"Why don't you come pick me up at the Starbucks across the street? I'll get us some coffee and breakfast for the road," she said.

"What? You're not interested in the free breakfast here?" he countered with a grin.

She made a noise and held the back of her hand in front of her mouth. "Gah, I just threw up a little in my mouth."

"I'm guessing the bathroom would be cleaner there too," he said, grabbing his jacket. "I'll be there as soon as I can."

They left the room together, leaving the key in the room. No sense reintroducing themselves to jack-off guy, or worse, a day manager who actually watched the news instead of porn.

He left Casey as she crossed the road, and retraced their steps a few blocks in the opposite direction. Then he stuck out his hand and hailed one of the many cabs making their early morning pilgrimage to McCarran Airport. He got out at the terminal, tipping the driver just enough that he'd be happy, but not enough that he'd remember his passenger later.

At the arrivals area, he hopped the bus to long-term parking. As the bus pulled away, leaving him in the remotest part of the parking lot, he swiped his foot over his shoelaces, unfastening one.

He walked to where dozens of people were leaving their cars and herding families toward the different bus stops. He'd already figured a family minivan would be the best choice, and he spotted a harried-looking man dropping his wife, two kids, and all the luggage at one of the bus stops.

God bless him, he was headed to a less-full part of the parking lot. Cameron bent to tie his shoelaces as he watched him park and slip the parking ticket into his blazer pocket. Too easy. Now he wouldn't even have to lose the ticket. He watched for that sweet spot—the second the guy relaxed. He'd got his car parked, his family was at the bus stop.

Come on. Come on. His ruse really wouldn't work as well

if he didn't relax. Then the man smiled a tiny smile to himself and his shoulders dropped. That was it.

Cameron jumped to his feet and rushed at the man from behind a Ford truck. "Excuse me. I've lost my…have you seen two little girls? One this high—" He held his hand at waist height. "And one about this high?" He held his hand much lower. Then he crumpled his face. "I don't even remember what they were wearing. What kind of father am I?"

The man instantly went on alert and looked around, even standing on tiptoes to see over the cars. Cameron slipped his hand into the man's pocket and slid out the ticket.

"I'm sorry, I haven't seen them." He looked anxiously at his own family. "Can I help you look—" the man started.

Cameron's heart dropped a tiny bit, and suddenly he hated his training. He hated how instinctively he knew how to appeal to this particular man. He hated that he was going to steal his car. He looked around the parking lot, and gasped, pressing his hand to his heart and letting out a huge sigh. "Oh, thank God. Look. There they are." He pointed in toward a disparate group of people leaving cars and dragging luggage out of trunks. He bent and braced his hands on his knees in apparent relief.

The man clapped him on his back. "Don't worry, buddy. It happens to all of us."

"Thank you. Oh, man…the bus!" He pointed at the bus heading toward the bus stop where the man's family stood.

"Gotta run!" the man said happily, before jogging over to the stop.

Cameron just stood and watched him go. Why hadn't he

picked on an ass to scam? He'd never used his training in the U.S. Never had to victimize anyone other than an enemy of the state. He felt like shit. He took a moment to ask forgiveness from the universe, and ducked behind a car to wait for the bus to take away the long line of travelers at the bus stop.

They had a car now. A nice, suburban-style family car that wouldn't attract any attention. It was the right thing to do. They were on the run. They were in danger. At least Casey was. Pilots were missing, and dammit, this was the right thing to do. As much as he hated to admit it, Casey was right. He was leaving this van as pristine as he found it.

Damn her. And damn him. He hoped karma wouldn't come back and kick his ass.

# CHAPTER 7

Before heading into Starbucks, Casey popped into the Walgreens next door and picked up deodorant, a T-shirt that had VEGAS decaled over the chest, and some sweatpants-shorts that were the only items of clothing they had for a lower half that weren't made for a three-year-old. It would do until she got to a proper store.

She also picked up some PowerBars and bottles of water. And then—why not—a huge bottle of wine for $4.99. Bound to have an elegant bouquet, but she figured by the end of the day—if they made it that far—they wouldn't care how cheap it was. If she was honest, she wouldn't really care at the best of times either.

Instinctively she shoved a first-aid kit into her basket from the display next to the cashier. She left with three bags and an overwhelming desire for coffee. Lots of coffee. She bought two thermal cups, and had the barista fill them with two regular coffees, and also bought two more, to drink as soon as Cameron returned.

As the young woman was filling her order, she slipped into the bathroom and changed, washing as much of herself as she could with hand soap and paper towels. At least she felt as if she'd cleaned off the worst of the room gunk that she imagined had settled on her skin.

She wondered what she looked like to passers-by. Sneakers, vacation T-shirt, impossibly tight, small shorts that she had to pull down to cover her back-side, and a handful of plastic bags, along with her Jimmy Choo handbag. The road was getting busy with commuters already, and she guessed that made it better for them. More cars meant less visibility.

Still he didn't come. A finger of anxiety poked her already acidic stomach. Maybe he'd changed his mind and gone back to base. Maybe he'd got caught stealing a car. Maybe he'd boosted a car, and had an accident on the way back to her. Maybe...her thoughts were interrupted by the honk of a horn.

She blew out a breath of relief when she saw him at the wheel of a silver minivan. She smiled as he jumped out. "Nice outfit," he said with a grin.

"The shop assistant said it was a classic combination of a high-price hooker and spring-breaker? Was she right?" Casey said, fluttering her eyelashes.

He looked her up and down for a second. "She certainly...hit the nail on the head there."

Casey rolled her eyes with a laugh

"We'll be on the road for a while. If memory serves, any-

way. It's been ten years since I've been there." He took the
bags she was carrying and slid the rear door open to throw
them in. The wine bottle clunked against the carpet. He
raised his eyebrow.

"Just in case we needed a distraction from the hole I put
us in," she explained.

"It's not Jim Beam, by any chance?" he asked.

She hated to dash his hopes. "Not exactly. But I'm sure
it works the same way." She fished around in the bag and
showed him.

He winced. "It'd better."

She got in the driver's seat. "So, we're heading east right?
Toward Connecticut at least?"

He put his seat belt on in silence, and then turned in his
seat. "Not exactly."

She took a breath. She had to trust him. But that familiar
chill up her spine reminded her that regardless of who was in
the car with her, she was in this alone. Sure, she was putting
her trust in Cameron, but she could cut and run as soon as
she needed to if she thought he had his own agenda.

"So where to?" she asked, putting the coffees in the various cup holders. She couldn't help but see the comfort in
having a minivan. Cup holders, what looked like a built-
in fridge, a DVD player in the back. She wondered what
movies they had stashed away.

And then she kicked herself. She was beginning to think
that her brain was tricking her into thinking about irrelevan-
cies so that she didn't completely melt down. Maybe it was
right. Maybe she should think about fucking cup holders,

and movies, and what she looked like in her stupid shorts, and jumping Cameron, when all else failed her.

Maybe that was better than the alternative.

There was silence in the car. She looked at Cameron and he was looking quizzically at her.

"What?" she asked.

"You haven't been listening to anything I've been saying, have you?"

Shit. What had he said. "Sure I have. You just told me where we were going, is that right or left out of here?" She hurriedly pulled toward the entrance of the parking lot.

"I asked you which was my coffee," he said, punctuating his words as if she were a child.

Fuck, she didn't even care. "They're all lattes. I figured we could do with the extra protein."

"Yeah, but I drink only soy decaf lattes with a double espresso shot, extra foam and extra hot, with cinnamon sprinkled on top, but no chocolate."

"What?" She jammed on the brake.

He drank from his coffee. "We're taking the 95 toward Tonopah. Good thing I'm not lactose intolerant or anything."

She wanted to hit him, to say something clever, yet biting. But she needed coffee before her brain was sharp enough for that. "What's in Tonopah?"

"Nothing as far as I know. We'll then need the 376 toward Manhattan, Nevada, and then after an hour or so, I'm going to have to rely on my memory to find the place."

"Yeah, but what place?"

"I'd rather not say until we get there. I don't want you overthinking it," he said, and then took another gulp of coffee.

"Stop treating me like a child," she said.

"Drink your coffee—then we'll talk. I'm worried about you. You're zoning out when I'm talking, and you're really easily distracted. Oh my God, look at the size of that squirrel!" He pointed out of the window.

She tapped the brake to slow down and see what he was talking about. There was nothing.

"You see? We're on a Cannonball race across the country, probably with bad guys behind us, and you're slowing down to look at squirrels. What's happened to the crack pilot who routinely risked her life for people she didn't even know? What happened to you be being ready at any time of the day or night to jump into your MJ-130J?"

She took several sips of her coffee, trying not to blow up at the man who had basically volunteered to help her. "Have you ever had anyone after you? I mean you personally. Not you the special operator? Because it's different when it's you. When it's personal.

"Every time my brain slows down, every time the adrenaline trickles away, I'm left picturing my life in prison. Or being killed by the sociopathic security chief at TGO. I would've died for my country in a heartbeat. But I am not dying for the sake of company secrets." She shrugged. "You still see this as a mission. For me it's my life. And if it's distracting me, you're going to have to live with that."

"Fair enough," he said mildly. Infuriatingly.

After about five hours droning down Route 95, they stopped and switched drivers. And not a second too soon. Casey looked as if she was ready to pass out at the wheel. Oh, she insisted that she was fine, but after one too many veers onto the shoulder, he ordered her into the backseat to sleep. Besides which, they needed gas.

They set off again with burgers in their bellies, Casey in the rear, and a niggling feeling that something wasn't right. But in truth he didn't even know if he could trust his gut at this stage. His hands were still sore from hitting the men in the parking lot, and that alone served as a stark reminder that he'd left his special operator days, and training, way behind him.

And yet here he was, on a mission—Casey had been right about that. It was just a mission to him. Sure he took it personally that two pilots had crashed during his exercise, but it wasn't actually personal. He didn't *know* the pilots. This was a duty, more than anything else.

And the problem with that was that they didn't have any matrices for success. When he was in the Special Operations Wing, every day he went hot, he knew what the mission was, and what success looked like, what sacrifices they'd be willing to make, and what the backup plans were.

And now he was risking his own life, taking a TGO employee to a secret place that she had no business knowing about. He wanted to trust her, but he was worried about what she wasn't telling him. Worried that somehow, what she was keeping secret could affect how they approached this mission. She wouldn't tell him what was in her safe, and he couldn't assess if whatever was in there could stop TGO from causing any more accidents. Everything was a big fat mess in his brain.

He looked in the rearview mirror at Casey. She was lying across the first row of seats, her head on some kind of Incredible Hulk blanket. Her mouth was open, and he was pretty sure that if he checked back in ten minutes, she'd be drooling.

Truth was, he needed a rest too. He wasn't firing on all cylinders, and—huh? He looked in the rearview mirror again, and his heart rate kicked up. There was an SUV behind them. The road they were on was a pretty straight road, not much ahead, and he knew there'd been nothing behind them when he'd just looked at Casey.

"Casey? Casey!" he shouted.

Her head popped up, and before she could open her mouth to ask why he was shouting at her, a bullet shattered the rear window. "Stay down!" he yelled.

"You think?" she shouted back.

The minivan jerked as the SUV hit its bumper. "Shit. What have we got in the back there?" he asked, knowing it was useless to hope for a weapons cache, shoulder missile launcher, or a grenade.

Casey wriggled onto the floor and flipped half of the first row of seats down. Then she climbed through to the second row, and eyed the contents of the way-back. "A collapsed stroller, a spare tire under the floor, a jack, and a box of canned goods. Looks like they forgot to stop off at the food bank."

"You want to drive or throw?" he asked, wondering why the hell there weren't police on this fucking road. Or other traffic. Where was everyone?

"If you'd ever seen me play softball, you'd want me to drive," Casey said, jerking halfway through the sentence as the car behind hit them again.

He undid his seat belt. "Get up here if you can. It's on cruise control," he said.

She crawled fast through the car, staying as low as she could. He carefully extricated himself from the seat into the passenger seat, keeping a hand on the wheel. The car jerked again as the bastard tried to force them off the road.

Casey clambered in a lot more efficiently than he had got out. "You want me to try to outrun him? Or...?"

"I don't know yet. Just keep it steady." He slid into the rear of the car. It looked as if there were only two people in the SUV. "These people *really* hate you," he shouted.

She didn't reply, so he started throwing cans through the shattered back window. Talk about freaking high-tech fighting. Chickpeas and baked beans. They didn't cause any damage, but it had made them hang back a little instead of sitting on their bumper. The spare tire would fuck them up, if he could get it through their windshield. If he could throw it from the back of their van without getting shot.

He had a flashback to staking out an Iraqi market, with no weapons and no radio, watching for a suicide bomber. He'd found him, caught him, and disabled him before any backup had arrived. Fuck this shit. He wasn't fighting from a fucking car.

"Pull over," he yelled.

"What?" Casey yelled back. "Are you nuts?"

"Nope, I've just come to my senses. Pull over. Take an exit if you can. This one." He pointed at a sign for a town he'd never heard off. He noticed that she used her indicator to take the exit. He made a mental note never to tap her to be a getaway driver.

She pulled off the road and unfastened her seat belt.

"Wait." His mind was whirring. "Okay, run out of the car toward them, pretend I've kidnapped you and you're happy to see them. That should put them off guard for a moment. I'll do the rest."

"Should? Why aren't they going to shoot me on sight?" she asked, panic infusing her voice.

"Mostly, those shorts and that top. No man is going to shoot you on sight. Fact."

"What if it's a woman?"

He had nothing. "You'll think of something."

She paused, then nodded. "Okay, I've got this."

He crouched on the floor of the van as she screamed, stuck her hands out of the window, and then opened the car door. Both men were out of their SUV with their weapons drawn. "Are you TGO?" she shouted. "Oh, thank God. The man in there kidnapped me. Please help me!"

In the side mirror he saw the men look at each other, confused. Casey pressed home the advantage by running toward them with her hands raised. "You're here to rescue me? Oh, thank God! You shot him. He's in the back. Please help me!"

The man on the right of the car raised his weapon and

approached the minivan. Clearly he had no idea how to approach a suspect vehicle. And thank Jesus for the tinted windows. The man put his hand on the handle and leaned in to slide the door open. As Cameron crouched on the floor, he half-smiled to himself and used all his force to open the door. The TGO guy lost his balance and virtually fell on Cameron. It was easy to take the gun from his hand and push him onto his ass.

Cameron jumped out of the car and approached his would-be assailant. With one punch to the nose, he eliminated the threat. He jumped up, worried that it had taken him too long to neutralize his guy. That worry doubled when he saw Casey struggling to disarm her attacker.

Cameron was about to step in when Casey said "Oh for God's sake," kicked him in the knee, and neatly took his gun while flipping him over her shoulder. Cameron ground to a halt and winced as the man collapsed, screaming.

"Nice job," he said as she checked the safety and tucked it into the waistband of her absurdly sexy shorts.

Jesus, he wanted her like hell. Her face was sweaty, standing over an enemy with his gun in her pants. Her hair was all mussed up from the fight. He wanted her right now.

She crouched next to the man, and he had to look away, as he was 100 percent sure that if he continued to look, he would be able to see up her shorts.

"Who sent you?" she asked him.

The guy's teeth were grinding too hard with pain to answer her. Cameron approached him and kicked his thigh, close enough to the groin that the man turned away, his hands cupping his nuts. "Okay, okay. Grove sent us. You are just a loose end. That's what he said."

Casey's breath started coming hard and fast as she stood and took a step back.

"Get in the car, Casey. I'll drive," he said. He worried that she was going into shock, or panic, or something. "Casey," he repeated when she didn't even look at him.

She snapped her attention to him. "Yes, sir." She turned and went directly to the passenger seat, as if she were taking orders from a superior officer.

That was weird.

Cameron wanted to ask the guy a hundred questions. He also had an unbearable urge to kill him, but he knew he couldn't. He looked at the man. "So, what happens now?" he asked.

"They send someone worse. Much worse."

"How did you find us?" he asked.

The man was silent but held up his hand in surrender as Cameron advanced on him again. "We've been tracking her phone."

Fury bubbled up in him. What kind of amateur…? He looked back at the car. She fucking took him on the run and still had her fucking phone with her? His fists clenched. What was *wrong* with her?

He couldn't even talk to her when he got back in the car. But he turned and drove them back the way they'd come from before. "Where are we going?" and then she looked behind her. "Do you think we should have left water for them?"

"Are they your friends, Casey? Shall we go back with a gift card to urgent care too?"

She turned and just stared at him. He took his eyes off the road for a moment to stare back.

It was already getting dark. It felt like they'd been on the road for hours already. He pulled off the road and drew up to a large barn with no houses around it. "Would you be so kind as to give me the TGO phone they've been tracking us on?" he said, trying not to shout.

She paled. "Oh my God," she whispered. She stared at him for a second and then scrambled in the back for her phone. "I can't believe…I'm so sorry." She handed him the phone. He stalked over to the barn and broke a small old window. He lobbed the phone inside as far as it would go.

He was almost shaking with anger. *Stay calm. Stay calm.*

They got back on the road, and back in the right direction. Hopefully if anyone was still tracking it, it would buy them some time as they descended on the abandoned barn. Dammit. He should have taken it and thrown it in the back of the SUV that had followed them. They'd have been chasing each other for a few hours. See? Fucking losing his edge. He punched the steering wheel. Dammit. He was angry with her and with himself.

"I'm sorry. I didn't think about it after they tried to grab me. I forgot about the phone." She said. "Why didn't they come get us at the hotel last night?"

He took a breath. "There's a difference between having a shootout in a downtown Vegas hotel and being shot in the middle of nowhere, with no witnesses and limited chance of anyone finding our bodies." TGO had waited. They knew that Casey couldn't fly without tipping everyone off, so the only option open to her was to drive away. All they'd had to do was track and wait. It was what he would have done. It was what any tactical military person would have done.

He applied the brake and pulled over off the highway onto a dusty road.

"What? What is it?" she asked with a nervousness in her voice. She looked behind them, but there was nothing for her to see except darkness.

"Give me your things. Everything. I need to know what you've got on you. If I'm taking you to a place where we can be safe, I need to know that you're not fucking bringing everyone with us," he ground out.

"I may have fucked up, but I'm not that much of an amateur," she said, which pretty much just made him see red.

He nodded. "Get out of the car."

He didn't know what he was doing, or what he was thinking. But he needed to know that she wasn't endangering them. That she wasn't carrying a tracking device on her. Or any kind of wire, even a set of remote car keys. His whole brain was foggy, and it was making him paranoid. He could feel it, and objectively understand why, but his body wouldn't listen, and was already stoked on adrenaline.

The still, cool night air soothed him a bit. He took some deep breaths, hoping that Casey wouldn't see how tense he was.

*Maybe you've lost your edge?* His head told him. *Maybe you don't know anything anymore.* What the fuck was happening to him? When had he ever doubted his judgment or abilities. It was Casey. It had to be. He'd read her records, replayed her missions in his head, listened in when he knew she was flying. She was fucking with his brain, now.

Dragging him back into his past. A past he wasn't sure he was still equipped to manage. To see her walk into his life again after all those years had done something to the core of him. To his very essence. His head and instinct were fighting for supremacy inside him. She'd been part of his imagination for so long, and here she was, in danger, and he'd walked right into it with her. He'd trusted that she'd have at least a minimum of fucking sense. He was just fucked all the way around.

He needed to get his shit in control.

"Show me your bag," he demanded.

She leaned in the car to grab it, handed it to him without a word, and watched as he emptied the contents onto the hood of the car. In the dim light she winced as she took in the damage to the car. She took a shaky breath. "I'm sorry, Cameron. I didn't think…"

"That might be the first true thing you've told me."

# CHAPTER 8

*What?* "Dick," she muttered. He ignored her and kept pawing through her bag, as if the answer to the universe was in there. She'd been worried at his sudden anger, but now he was just being a douche.

He examined each item that had fallen out of her bag, and then felt his way through the tan leather bag itself. There was nothing there. It was a Jimmy Choo. Just acknowledging that she'd paid thousands of dollars for a freaking handbag made her realize just how crazy her life had become after she'd been recruited at TGO. She'd been paid so much money, she could afford multiple Jimmy Choos. Surely that should have tipped her off that something wasn't right. Had they started buying her off right from her very first paycheck? The thought made her feel queasy, and she rubbed her stomach as she watched him check a tube of lipstick, a small container of tampons, and a couple of stray condoms that had been at the bottom of her handbag for who knows how long. She wasn't embarrassed, and he didn't seem to be either.

"Now it's your turn," he said, his voice hard, but more strained than angry.

"What now?" she replied, startled.

Before she'd finished asking the question, his hard hands were on her shoulders. It surprised her into silence. For a second, she wanted to close her eyes and just feel him touching her. Suddenly, the years of longing for him, then not seeing him for months, only for the feeling to return whenever he popped back on to base, came front and center.

She forced herself to say something. "What are you doing?" She even managed to inject an indignant tone into her voice. She was pretty proud of that.

He paused as his hands squeezed the T-shirt she'd bought that morning "I mean no disrespect, but I really don't trust you. I have two missing—possibly dead—pilots, and I have you. You were in the control room when word came in about the crash. You had the guiltiest look on your face as you left the room. You, who still look guilty. I'm prepared to give you the benefit of the doubt, since I saw someone try to grab you. But now I just don't know.

"Our date you skipped out on, after being careful to drive very slowly past the officers' club parking lot? Suspicious. Everything is suspicious to me right now. So yes, I'm going to frisk you for anything your company can use to track us. And you're going to stand there and take it." His expression was grim.

"Seriously? You're suspicious of *me*? You *know* me," she

said, playing for time. She had nothing to hide, but the fact that she was now on the run with the man of her dreams who inexplicably seemed to think that she was a bad dude, made her nervous.

He took a half step back, but it wasn't enough to calm her racing heart. "Correction: I *knew* you. Kind of." He frowned to himself, and she wondered what he was thinking. "I slightly knew you." He countered.

"What?" She had no idea what he was doing, but he seemed to be talking himself out of the fact that he'd known her for years. Sure, they hadn't talked a lot, but her crew had told her that he'd always been in the control room when she flew. She'd seen it as a good luck charm. That someone of his legendary skills was looking out for her and her crew. Of course, she guessed that could have been crap. Maybe it had been his job to be there, or maybe it had been a coincidence that he'd been there for all her missions. Had she been fooling herself this whole time? Maybe he'd never thought about her after Afghanistan. But then she remembered…

"It was a date?" She pressed her lips together to stop herself from smiling.

"What?"

"Every time you've mentioned the officers' club, you've called it a date. We were going on a date." What was she doing? Embarrassing him, or goading him into action? Then she felt her half-smirk fade from her face. She was being stupid. He was literally backing away from her. Physically and mentally. Saying he didn't really know her. That he thought she was complicit somehow with TGO, which in a way she was. Although she didn't know what TGO actually was doing. Had it been a terrible error that they put the wrong version of the software on the planes? Or had it been done deliberately?

"Can I ask you a question?" she asked.

"I don't know, can you?" he replied, like an ass.

"Did my company put software of any kind on the aircraft at Red Flag? Was that part of the sponsorship deal?"

Cameron took another step back, anxiety and anger fighting for dominance in his expression. "No. You know that would be a nonstarter. We don't do after-market alterations on aircraft unless we've seen the testing and think that it's a legit improvement on what we've got. After-market add-ons don't usually have a great track record. As well you know. So, what are you saying?" His voice was getting louder. "Are you telling me that your company fucked with the aircraft at Red Flag?"

*Shit. No. Backtrack. Backtrack.* But even before she said the words, she knew she'd hesitated too long for it to be plausible. "I'm not saying that at all!" she said. *Because if I did, I'd be going to jail. If she wasn't already dead.* Damn the nondisclosure, and damn Malcolm for telling her about James Turner. If he hadn't mentioned that the previous whistle-blower had been sued successfully and then "died," she wouldn't have hesitated to tell Cameron everything she knew, or suspected. But her sense of self-preservation, and her need to find out what really happened and to protect Cameron who had already gotten himself involved by saving her, overrode everything.

"Then why are you asking me?"

"I…I can't tell you that," she squeaked, and then cleared her throat. She hadn't thought that one through. Of course he'd have a follow-up. She had to tell him what was going on. Not the facts, just the reason why she couldn't tell him.

"Give me a reason not to take you back to base. Because if you don't tell me what happened to those two pilots and their aircraft, I will kill you myself." He was practically radiating fury, and God help her, she found it pretty hot. That probably didn't speak well of her.

She stayed silent.

He lunged forward and grabbed her shoulders. *Kiss me. Kiss me,* her whole body shouted silently. But instead he pulled her arms out to the side.

"Seriously?" she asked.

"Spread them," he commanded.

She tried to keep her face neutral, and said "Yes, sir!" as she assumed the position. She opened her legs and spread her arms like she'd done a hundred times for the TSA when traveling.

And then he hesitated. With that hesitation, came a sense of power, a feeling that he was tacitly accepting that touching her was not going to be a regular TSA frisk.

Her skin tingled with the breeze, and the anticipation of his touch. She rose an eyebrow at him. "Well come on then, Commander. Make sure I'm not a bad guy."

What had started off as a run-of-the mill frisk—one he'd done a thousand times with every person he allowed on his aircraft—had turned into something else entirely. But dammit, he wasn't going to let her think he was fazed. He grabbed her shoulders and roughly jerked her nearer to him. She complied without a sound.

He dug his fingers into the soft part of her shoulder again. If he was being honest with himself, he was giving her shoulders more of a massage than anything else.

He briskly moved down her arms. He thought he was moving briskly, but in reality his touch lingered. The T-shirt she wore was thin, so it was almost like he was touching her skin. He swallowed and tried to concentrate on ensuring she had no weapons or…yeah. He wasn't fooling anyone. He could see fairly easily that she wasn't packing. True, he was a little nervous about being set up by TGO, but there was no way a military hero like Casey would do that. He hoped.

She raised an eyebrow at him again and he realized his hands had all but stopped moving on her arms. He cleared his throat and continued.

And then he remembered what happened next after the torso. Ankles, and legs. Of course, with the shorts she was wearing, he didn't need to do her legs.

Every molecule of his body insisted. Blood started flowing around his body, but unfortunately not to his brain.

He hesitated, needing some control, or barring that, someone to beat some sense into him before he totally lost his head. What the hell was he thinking?

"Cat got your…?" Her sentence trailed off suggestively, at least to his ears.

*Tongue. Tongue. Tongue.* Damn, this was all wrong. He

tried to put his thoughts in a lockbox, but there was no box strong enough to withstand the years he'd spent thinking about her.

He slid his hands down her arms, and back up. Goddamn it. It was like she was daring him. He swallowed hard as he ran his fingers over her collarbone, and then down the center of her chest.

The flutter of her breath touched his cheek as he leaned over her. Her arms and legs still spread for him, it was as if she were surrendering to him. Before his raging hard-on made him do something they'd regret, he searched her face for consent.

Her eyes met his, and then trailed down his face to his mouth. As he watched her, her lips parted beneath his gaze. His whole consciousness was a mass of heat and need and longing. He bent to claim her lips but paused a hair's breadth away from her mouth, needing her to make the reach, to assure him that she wanted the same thing.

She stretched a bare centimeter toward him, and he took possession of her. His mouth touched hers and fucking fireworks exploded inside him. Those nights, those long missions, just thinking about the brave, fearless pilot he'd encountered so many times before. His.

Casey's heart nearly stopped beating with the relief, need, anticipation of his kiss. She'd never allowed herself to be vulnerable to anyone, but having the man of her daydreams frisk her on the side of the road was too much for any woman.

She lost herself in the heat of his mouth and the demand of his tongue.

She wrapped her arms around his shoulder to get closer, but he pulled away. "Did I say you were at ease?" he asked.

"No, sir," she said, slowly holding her arms up again. What was he doing? Confusion fused in her brain.

He felt his way along her arms again, this time not stopping. His hands moved firmly across her collarbone, and straight down to her breasts. His touch lingered, and Casey held her breath. He dragged his hands over them, once, twice…and then rubbed his thumbs across her nipples. She gasped as they became hard under her T-shirt.

"I didn't give you permission to speak either," he said.

For a second, Casey snapped back to being a subordinate officer, but her aching nipples told her that this was some kind of test. Or role-play. Or…she didn't care what it was—she was so wet from wanting him, that she was just thankful they were on a totally deserted road, because if he ordered her to strip, so help her, she would.

He continued his "frisk," running his hands over her tight belly and around to her ass. She bit her lip. *Touch me. Touch me.*

But his hands swept down her legs until he crouched at her ankles, running his fingers over the black high-heeled sandals she was wearing. Then he started his journey back up. His hands passed along her naked legs, which obviously didn't need frisking, over her knees right up to her edge of the shorts. *Touch me. For the love of God, touch me.*

"Turn around, and face the car," he barked.

She took a sharp breath, lowered her eyes, and slowly turned around.

A whispering touch flickered at her side, and she realized that he was raising her T-shirt. Every rationalization that had permeated her foggy brain dissipated in a rush. He wasn't frisking her. *He isn't frisking me.* And Jesus, even if he was, this was the hottest she'd ever been in her life. Ever.

He pulled the T-shirt off her, barely touching her at all. It was as if it were falling off by its own accord. By magic. She opened her eyes and looked up at the sky as she bit back a moan. The sky was completely black save the stars and the half-moon that hid behind some tall pines. The air was cool but not cold, and she was in her bra at the side of the road.

To say her life had changed within the past twenty-four hours would be a small understatement. But damn, if it hadn't shown her how fleeting life and normality could be. She wanted to embrace everything different, and new, and exciting. And Cameron was all of these things. Heat buzzed around her body, making her insides feel like fire, and her skin chilled in the night air. The combination of feelings set her heart pumping and made her breath come in heavy gasps that she tried to stifle.

"Put your hands on the hood," Cameron growled.

His hands encircled her waist for a second, and then he pulled her shorts down to her feet and threw them to the side. He nudged her legs farther apart. Jesus. Please don't let him see how wet her panties must be. He dragged his hands up her legs again, right to the top, then he bunched her panties in his fist, and yanked them upward, putting and almost unbearable strain on her clit.

She arched her back instinctively, relishing the friction. His teeth bit her bare ass cheek, and burning with the need to feel anything, she arched farther, pressing her ass more firmly against his teeth. He drew back, and for a long second, she couldn't feel him touch her anywhere. The anticipation clenched inside her, every part of her tightened.

Then he released her bra. She raised her hands from the car to allow it to fall off, into the sand on the ground. She really wanted to turn around. To make him look at her. She worked hard at keeping her body military-fit. She was proud of its lines and strength. But she didn't want to break the spell.

"I bet you're used to hiding things in unconventional places, aren't you? Damned contractors are all the same," he whispered in her ear.

If she hadn't been on the verge of exploding, she would have taken issue with that, but she was. "Yes, sir," she breathed out more as a whisper.

With her admission, his cool hands slipped around her and grabbed the door of the car, forcing her to bend farther over, bracing herself with her hands. At the same time his foot kicked her legs farther apart. She couldn't have been more vulnerable if she tried.

He seemed happy with her position, so he straightened, but not before she felt his huge hard-on press against her. She moved her hips infinitesimally to feel a little friction, but he jerked away and slapped her ass.

"Ow," she gasped, with shock.

"Don't make me hurt you, Major," he said, with a clear grin in his voice.

She was getting so hot with this fucking role-play. "Yes, sir. I mean, no, sir."

With his feet pressing her legs open again, his hands slipped around her and cupped her breasts, immediately squeezing her already hard nipples, making her shudder with need.

She arched upward, needing more contact, needing something more than what he was offering. But he stepped away again.

She groaned. "Permission to speak freely, sir?" she asked.

"Granted." But as he said the words, his right hand dived between her legs, pulling the yanked up panties away and gently stroking her through them, a feather-light touch that served only to make her crazier with need for him. She closed her eyes and visualized him as she'd always seen him in Afghanistan: dirty, exhausted, sitting alone in the chow hall. Her fantasies had always had her seducing him right there, on the table, in front of everyone. Or outside, in the mountains, or on his Osprey...or in that bunker. In truth, she'd already fucked him nearly everywhere in her daydreams. But never had her fantasies come close to this. She needed him to touch her. Touch her properly, with purpose. She needed a release, and if she didn't get one soon, she was going to lose her mind.

"Turn around," he commanded.

She was about to refuse, when he picked her up and spun

her around, planting her ass on the hood of the car. "The only correct answer for you is 'Yes, sir,'" he said, pushing her up on the hood so her legs dangled off. She gasped as he yanked her panties off her, leaving her completely naked in front of him, and God, and any passer-by who happened to be taking the back roads to Vegas. *Fuck, that was hot*.

Before she could really complete her thought, he parted her legs and dipped his fingers between them into her wetness.

At last. She moaned and pressed against him, reveling in the sensation of him stroking her clit. She was so close to coming, but she wanted this…victory over her fantasies to last longer. But then he dipped his head and pulled her closer to him, holding her legs on his shoulders. *Jesus*. She collapsed back onto the warmth of the hood.

His tongue was hot against her, flickering at her clit, before flat tonguing her, and then licking all the way down to her ass, and then back again, only to deftly circle her again, bringing her almost immediately to the edge of her climax. She tried to wait, tried to prolong it, but the sensations were too much to bare. She closed her eyes and visualized him doing this in front of everyone in the chow hall. Her stomach clenched as she flew over the edge, and he slid his fingers inside her, feeling her orgasm as it crashed over her.

She gasped out loud, heaving breaths that she had trouble keeping up with. She was flying. As her tremors subsided, she opened her eyes, looking for his. Looking for a connection. Looking for something.

He smiled his cocky smile at her, his fingers still buried

deep inside her still. He curled them, and she jumped, feeling both too tender to come again, yet too turned on by the whole situation to want to stop. She reached behind her to where he'd dumped out her purse and grabbed one of the two condoms. She opened it with her teeth, not taking her gaze from his, and handed it to him.

He undid his belt and pulled his jeans down. Clearly he was a commando in more ways than one. His dick sprang free, and with one swift movement he slipped it on. He pulled her off the hood and spun her roughly around, pushing her back down, so she was offering everything to him. She felt his fingers first, playing around her clit again, starting her engine once again.

He positioned his dick at her entrance, and she strained backward to try get him inside her, but he resisted until she relaxed again, and then, with one thrust, he filled her totally.

She gasped with the intensity that flashed through her.

One of his hands snaked around her and held her left breast, squeezing and releasing her nipple, and the other went around her hips, stroking her clit in rhythm with his thrusts.

She was losing her mind. She pushed back against him, making him squeeze her nipple harder. She cried out in need and pain, her second orgasm building fast beneath his hands. As she opened her legs farther, to give him greater access, and greater depth, she heard a far-off rumbling in her ears. As she visualized him fucking her, she was consumed with the desire to watch him come inside her. In the distance she saw headlights flashing as the oncoming vehicle went over the bumps in the road in the distance.

"Oh my God," she said.

He stopped moving. "You think I care about some stranger seeing me fuck you on your car?" he whispered, resuming his thrusts, and his clit-play. "You think it wouldn't turn you on more, to think of some stranger seeing the hottest thing you could possibly see? Seeing you completely naked? Do you think he might think it was a dream?" His voice lulled her, and his words turned her on. How did he know her so well?

His fingers easily worked her into a frenzy again, and she met him thrust for thrust, heat building inside as if she'd never had sex before…hell, never even been turned on before. She could feel her orgasm within reach, heard his breathing change.

The headlights grew bigger, and the car so close she swore she could hear its music. The thought of a stranger watching them fuck took her way over the edge, he groaned as he thrust in her, this time holding himself inside, as she felt him his dick jerk as he came. She nearly came, but the car was too close.

Cameron withdrew from her, picked her up, and fell with her, behind the car, seconds before it passed. She laughed, half with nervousness. "I never knew you were so…" she said, trying to catch her breath.

"I never knew you were so…either." He rolled her over so she was on her back. "You're beautiful, but you have a filthy mind," he said with a grin.

"I'm a pilot, what did you expect?" she said, with an openness that surprised her.

"I expect you to come," he whispered again. "I feel you missed out there."

Before she could protest, he gently opened her legs by stroking them apart this time. He shifted so he was facing her, his head on his propped-up hand. "I get to watch you come now," he murmured.

Her back arched as he touched her again—this time so gently, stroking again and again, until she gasped, on the precipice. He bent and she felt his warm mouth on her nipple. Over the edge she went, grasping at the sand beneath her hands.

For a second, she wanted to stay there, naked, on the side of the road, with no thoughts of TGO and her life being flushed down the drain. She looked at Cameron.

"Yeah I know. Reality is a bitch," he said, sighing and flipping on his back too.

Casey wanted to hold his hand, do something that would allow her to believe that their intimacy was…intimate, and not just a random, hot, encounter. But if she was being honest with herself, she didn't need his comfort. She needed his skills as a special operator.

She smiled to herself. He was some kind of a special operator on the side of the road, that was for sure. But real life permeated, and as much as she would have liked to pretend that it hadn't, lying at the side of the road, looking at the stars, was not going to get those pilots back, was not going to get her life back, and was certainly not going to nail fucking TGO to the tree. And she was determined to do all three.

With clarity, she understood what she needed to do. But first, they needed somewhere to spend the night. And she needed to find her panties.

# CHAPTER 9

Cameron examined the state map that had been tucked behind the passenger seat. It was over ten years old and looked like a kid had puked on it at one time, but the page he needed was untouched. Of course it was untouched. There was nothing where they were going. No town, no houses, no buildings, just rocks and a road. There was no reason a suburban family would have any need to examine a map of that area.

He opened the map out to the pages he needed, and tucked it down the side of his seat for later. Casey drove as they got back on the road silently. And headed toward their destination.

"You know, there's a point here—which, in my opinion, is already a tiny dot in our rearview mirror—where you have to put the personal shit aside," he said to Casey. "You need to switch the focus off yourself, and put it on the pilots who are lost and the planes that are at risk. I know you're in danger,

I know your life is probably fucked right now. But if we're going to do this, I need to know that you're prepared to go down fighting."

She didn't reply immediately. He wondered if she would blow up. He knew it was a big ask. But he also knew her military training wasn't that far behind her. A couple of years at best. He knew she could step up, he just needed to remind her that she had the balls to do it.

"I know," she said. "Tell me about them."

"About who?" He frowned.

"The missing pilots. What are they like?"

Relieved, he decided to be completely honest. "Major Eleanor Daniels is the best F-16 on the books. Everyone knows that. Even her father."

"General Daniels? I met him and Eleanor at the initial briefing," she said, her voice becoming more firm.

"Yes. I've got to be honest. I think he's up to his neck in TGO. Danvers certainly seemed to be in control of him," Cameron said, thinking back to the few interactions he'd seem them share.

"You think he'd be complicit in his daughter's...accident?" she asked.

"I don't think he's complicit, exactly, but he knows a lot more about what happened than he's letting on. Before we left, he'd given the order to arrest an F-15 weapons officer, Major Missy Malden. But I wondered about that. He put her in protective custody. I keep wondering if he did that to protect her from TGO or to allow TGO easy access to her. Right now, I can't say exactly where he stands, except to say that he's not innocent." His thoughts flipped to Major Malden and her F-15 pilot, Colonel Conrad, who had all but confessed to having an inappropriate relationship with her. Had it been his own fault that his Red Flag had been an unmitigated disaster this year? Or was it just that this was the only year when he was only nominally in command? In reality everything had been turned over to TGO. Maybe it was him.

"Tell me about Eleanor," she asked.

He wished he knew more. He wished he knew more about all the competing Red Flag pilots, but unless he literally bumped into them, he was working from their records. "As I said, she was the best pilot in her squadron. Don't get me wrong, the whole squadron is exceptional, but she seemed to be able to anticipate every aggressor's move. She had a light touch on the controls that her instructors were always impressed with, and really fast reflexes. If we don't find her, there will be a big hole in our F-16 capabilities."

"What was she like, personally?" Casey asked.

"I don't really know. There were multiple complaints about her on her file, but reading between the lines, as everyone before me obviously had, the complaints came from butt-hurt male colleagues."

"What do you mean 'as everyone obviously had'?"

"She kept getting promoted, even though a few guys in her squadron kept complaining that she was a careless pilot, that she took chances, that she was dangerous. Her record is clear on her ability, and her risk analysis. The complaints came from pilots who didn't like her becoming their leader. She didn't have many friends, but no one disliked her."

"What about the other pilot?"

"British. Flight Lieutenant Dexter "Ironman" Stone. This was his second crash."

"What? He crashed a plane and continued to fly? He must have balls of steel!" she exclaimed. She was right, though. Not many military pilots either lived to fly after a crash, or had the desire to fly after. "I guess. But his Typhoon was brought down by a shoulder-launched missile. He didn't exactly walk away—but as good as. He was also the best Typhoon pilot in the Royal Air Force. That's why he was at Red Flag. And not for nothing, that's why you were at Red Flag the times you competed there."

She swiveled her head to look at him. "What? I was only there as support."

"Every single pilot, from the helos doing search and rescue, to the Sentinels running surveillance, and the air traffic controllers, are hand selected. Your records were examined and you were an easy pick."

She frowned at him. "You're making that up. How would you even know? I never competed at Red Flag while you were commander there."

Shit. She had him. He either lies and tells her that he was lying to her to make her feel better, or he admits that he kept tabs on her and read her records every now and again. Fuck.

"I may have kept tabs on you after I got to Red Flag."

She grinned, and he wanted to punch himself. "So, you

pulled my files for no good reason when you became commander in Nellis?"

"Well since you dragged me into your life-or-death situation here, and we may not make it out alive—or sane—then, sure. If it makes you feel better, I was keeping tabs on you. Every now and then I'd wonder when you'd be back to Red Flag, but then I heard that you'd turned your papers in and traded it all for the money, and I never expected to see you again." He shrugged, as though the idea that he wouldn't ever see her again hadn't ripped him apart a little. Hadn't made him doubt his life choices, hadn't made him wonder if he should have put in a request to have her transferred to the Red Flag community earlier.

It hadn't been the end of his world, and he hadn't thought about her constantly, but it was more a niggle, that he'd missed out on...something.

"Aw, you're so cute. I wish I could take a photo of you right now," she said, seemingly ignoring the guilt he'd tried to lay on her.

"Shut up and drive," he growled.

The sun had risen and the heat was visibly shimmering above the quiet road. Years ago, this very situation could have been a part of one of his fantasies. Casey and he, on their way to a vacation. Time out of their busy military schedules. Hiding their relationship from anyone else, the fact that it had to be secret would have made it hotter for him, probably.

Fuck. He wished he could take back what they'd just done. He'd never needed anyone as strongly before, but it had been wrong. He wanted to seduce her in luxury—a five-star hotel somewhere quiet. Slowly taking her to the brink several times before letting her fly.

"Are you okay?" Casey frowned.

"Of course." He bristled, annoyance in his voice. "Why?"

"You groaned. Your eyes were closed. I wondered if you were in pain. I never noticed if you'd been hurt. Are you?"

"No." He tried to manufacture anger to keep a hard-on at bay. Damn. This whole thing—being with Casey, the tension between them, the men who were presumably after them—it was going to get messy, he could feel it in his bones.

And he realized now, that his bones were never wrong.

A couple of hours later, with their fuel gauge perilously low, he asked her to take an unmarked turn on the right. To Casey it looked as if they were headed toward the mountains, and it didn't look as if there was anything between them and the plateau ahead.

She guessed it'd be an ideal place to dump a body. She just hoped it wasn't hers. She smiled to herself. She wasn't sure why, but all her doubt about Cameron had disappeared. She wasn't sure if she truly harbored no concern that he'd turn her over to TGO, or that she was kind of beyond caring too much about it.

Casey was beginning to feel like a walking dead woman. She'd been driving a stolen car for three hours, she was on the run. There wasn't really an easy way to come back from that. She stole a glance at Cameron, who was peering intently out of the windshield, presumably looking for landmarks that he remembered.

"When was the last time you were here?" she asked, catching her breath as they bounced over a pothole. "There are more holes on this road than there is road."

"It's been over ten years, I'm sure. Stop!" His head swiveled to his right. "Go back. We need to take that road."

She slipped the car into reverse and hesitated at the place he pointed at. "That's not a road."

"Stop being such a lightweight," he grumbled as she yanked the steering wheel to make the turn.

They drove down toward a broken security gate and an old guardhouse without a roof. It was gray, but it was hard to tell if it had been painted that way, or just been beaten by the loose sand. The roof was lying alongside the house, as if a gust had blown it there. There was a one-bar barrier, that was neither up nor down, but stuck on a diagonal. She drove around it, because even though it clearly used to be a security check, there was no perimeter fence, or wall, or anything.

"It looks like it's been more than thirty years since anyone's been here," Casey said in a low voice.

Cameron just smiled and said nothing.

As they drove slowly away from the gate, she could see illuminated in their headlights that this place had once been an airstrip. They were on what looked like a taxiway. Or had once been a taxiway. The familiar airstrip signs were still there, pointing to runway 2-7, rusty and bent as if they were from a different era, but now it was just old concrete broken up by grass that over the years had pushed through the cracks.

There was one old hangar in a state of neglect similar to that of the guardhouse.

They pulled up to it and Casey's heart sank. It was deserted, no lights on anywhere. No sound, no people. The hangar had broken windows at the top, and the front door was wedged against the doorframe with a brick. It didn't feel like luck was on their side. Again.

"What are we going to do now?" she asked with a sigh.

Cameron clicked the button to release his seat belt, and didn't move. "Wind down your window and put your hands out." He proceeded to do the same.

"What? Are you nuts? Wait! Are the police here?" she looked anxiously around.

"Just do it!" he growled, hoping his intensity would motivate her to do as she was told.

She took the order and did as she was asked. "What is going on?" she asked between clenched lips, as if she was trying to talk without anyone seeing her actually say anything.

"Just give it a min—" His door was flung open from the outside and the muzzle of a shotgun poked into the car. It glinted in the moonlight.

For a long second, Casey was sure they'd had it. That TGO had caught up with them again, and that they'd die with Cameron thinking she'd led the bad guys to them again.

"Damn. Cameron? Duke Cameron? I nearly shot you for fuck's sake," a voice said.

"The fact that you didn't just shows that you've lost your edge," Cameron said.

"You fucker. Get on out here so I can kick your ass!"

Cameron laughed and got out of the car, leaving Casey inside, wondering what the hell was going on. The man hugged Cameron, nearly lifting him off his feet. "Come in, man." He nodded toward the hangar. "Bring your little lady too," he wisecracked.

"Little lady what?" Casey said, getting out of the car.

"Randy, meet Major Casey Jacobs—"

Randy dropped his shotgun to his side and snapped into a salute. "Ma'am."

"—retired," Cameron continued.

Randy dropped his salute. "Pleasure, ma'am."

"This is Chief Randy Angle," Cameron completed the introduction.

"Chief," Casey said with a nod. "Wait. Randy Angle? Is that your real name?" she looked quizzically at him.

"Sure is. It was either making a living in the military or as a porn star. I chose one as a career and one as a hobby."

Her mouth fell open.

"He's joking." Cameron grinned. Then he turned to Randy. "Wait, you *are* joking aren't you?"

# CHAPTER 10

Randy led them inside decrepit hangar, where they found another hangar. Casey stopped in her tracks as they both took in the vast difference between the outside hangar and the one inside. The walls were a polished white corrugated metal, and the door had a keypad and a thumbprint scanner.

"This is well hidden," Casey said in an impressed voice as he let them in to the inner sanctum.

"Randy likes his privacy," Cameron said. "Always has."

"That is the God's honest truth," Randy said, tucking his shotgun away in a gun rack with a considerable array of other weapons.

In front of them was a highly shined floor with three aircraft parked, nose to tail. To the right was an open-plan home, with a kitchen, living room, and metal stairs to a mezzanine floor that probably held his bedroom. It was a nice setup. Made Cameron's base housing look like shit. "Nice place, man. Really nice. You've made some improvements since I was last here."

"Thanks, brother." He nodded toward the large farmhouse table in the kitchen. "It's taken a bit of work, for sure."

Cameron held a chair for Casey, although she wasn't really paying attention, just looking around her new surroundings. "I want to live here. Can you build me one?" she asked.

Randy laughed, and put down three tumblers and a bottle of Jack. "What brings you to my humble abode?"

"As if anything about you could be considered humble," Cameron scoffed.

"It's true to say that my humility is a work in progress," he replied, taking a hit from the Jack, and leaning back in his chair, staring at Cameron.

Cameron looked at Casey, and though he was loath to pull in a favor this big, this was for Casey. She'd saved a lot of lives when she was in the air force. And as much as he wanted to protect her, he needed help. It was a life-changing admission for him. But he had the feeling that this whole situation would be life changing in one way or another.

Now they were both staring at him. Great.

"I'm invoking Warren Zevon," he said.

Totally different reactions flickered across their faces. Casey obviously didn't know what the fuck he was talking about, but Randy frowned, and then his face lit up as he realized what he was asking for.

"I am *stoked*!" Randy said, slamming his palm on the table.

"What? What are you talking about? Warren Zevon? Who's he? Can he—?" Casey began.

"'Lawyers, Guns, and Money,' baby!" Randy said with a whoop.

Casey slumped back in her chair watching the two of them high-five each other.

"So, what's going on, man? Everything I have is yours—you know that," his old friend said.

Cameron leaned forward and placed his hand briefly on Randy's leg in appreciation. "I know. We don't need everything you have…"

"I wouldn't mind this hangar," Casey said, with a shrug.

They both just looked at her. She held up both hands in surrender and let them continue.

"I heard about the accident, man. The press didn't mention any names. Was it anyone I know?" Randy asked.

Cameron sat back and took a sip of bourbon. "I don't think so. I don't know if you remember General Daniels?"

"I remember Colonel Daniels. He was kind of a jerk."

"He's General Daniels now, and his daughter Eleanor was one of the pilots."

Despite clearly having no time for General Daniels, he winced. "I never met her myself, but I heard she was a good pilot. She had the reputation for being a fighter."

"Yeah, she was. Is." Cameron berated himself for his slip in tense. Until he discovered differently, he was going to work under the assumption that both pilots were still alive. The fact that TGO couldn't find them meant that the company was inept, or the pilots had survived, and escaped. Although he knew the former was probably true, he was hanging on to hope that the latter was true as well.

"What you probably don't know, is that TGO—the military contractor—has taken over Red Flag this year. The government was going to cancel, so they stepped in to fund the whole program. But I'm suspicious that they had something to do with the crash, and they are trying to cover their tracks. Two pilots missing, one in detention, and they just tried to kidnap Casey here off base."

Randy nodded, processing the information. He talked with a slow southern drawl, and listened with wide eyes, as if he was struggling to take things in. Anyone who didn't know him might have thought his brain worked slow. But that couldn't be further from the truth.

"I heard on CNN that the vice president is throwing his confidence behind TGO," he said.

"Then you also heard that Casey and I are on some 'most wanted' list somewhere." Cameron took a swig of morning bourbon. It had been a long time since he'd drunk straight-up bourbon, and he had to confess that it was going down pretty well. He was safe here. Being here gave them time to think.

"Of course. Man, but Don Lemon doesn't seem to like you. I didn't want to say anything, because I thought it impolite. But yes. When I saw that, I figured it was only a matter of time before you showed up. Hoped anyway." He slapped the table again. "I'd just about given up hope of any excitement around here." His voice echoed around the huge space. "So, what's the plan?"

Cameron sat back in his chair and nodded toward Casey, who was swinging back on two chair legs, gazing up as if she'd never seen a ceiling before, clearly not listening to a word they were saying.

Randy looked at Cameron, and then back at Casey, and then back at Cameron, a smile twitching his mouth. Cameron shrugged and took another sip, then gave the table leg a good kick.

Casey jerked and grabbed the tabletop, a startled look on her face. "What?"

"Randy wants to know the plan."

"Right. Sure." She sat all four chair legs back down and nodded.

To Cameron's pleasure, she also took a gulp of Jack. "You want the whole story, Chief, or just the need-to-know stuff. I don't want to put you in any kind of danger here." Her gaze found Cameron's and he nodded.

Randy answered just about how Cameron expected him to. "Tell me everything. I'd kill for a little danger and intrigue."

"Crop dusting getting a little dull?" Cameron said, knowing full well that crop dusting wasn't exactly Randy's specialty.

"It's tough being the boss. Everyone else gets the exciting shit to do. I just stay here and make sure they get paid and have health insurance."

Cameron swiveled his head back to Randy. That didn't sound like crop dusting. He was running ops from here? He had employees? "Dude. You and I need to talk after we're done with this."

Randy grinned. "Yessir," he drawled, throwing a lazy salute across the table.

"As CNN told you, I worked for TGO. I suspect they are not on the up-and-up. I may have evidence that will at the very least, help the investigation into the crash—" She looked at Cameron. "Assuming we can get an independent inquiry even started." She turned back to Randy, who was listening intently. "But first two things need to happen. As I said, we need someone other than TGO to look at the crash—and so far all operating authority is with them. Secondly…" She cast a look in Cameron's direction again, this time a slightly more worried one. "…I need to make sure that passing the information to someone won't get me killed. Or jailed. And to do that, we need to get to Connecticut."

"Which aircraft do you want to take?" Randy asked. "And when?"

Casey was already on her feet. "Holy shit. I can fly one?" she asked, already headed back into the hangar area. "Will you marry me?" she added, over her shoulder.

"Yes, ma'am, I will," Randy drawled, eyes sparkling, watching her walk slowly around the planes, trailing her hand around the fuselage as if she were trying to seduce the damn thing.

Cameron jumped to his feet. Enough of that. "I'm flying. I'm probably the only one who is still licensed anyway, right?"

Randy swiveled back to him. His mouth dropped open. "Oh mah Gawd. It finally happened. You and…?" he whispered and nodded over his shoulder toward Casey.

"Shut up," Cameron ground out under his breath. "No. No to whatever you're thinking."

Randy whistled low. "Another pilot? You're in for an interesting life."

"I'm not…it's not. No. It's not like that. Back the fuck off." He stalked off as best he could on the shiny and slightly slippery hangar floor. But he realized he was smiling to himself.

"We'll take this one." He pointed at the Hawker.

"Good choice. You'll only have to refuel once, and you can use my fuel card so you don't have to use a credit card or anything. Let's get you some flight plans." Randy opened a cupboard and took out maps held together with rubber bands.

"You don't use online planners? iPads?" Casey asked, walking back to the kitchen table.

Cameron exchanged a look with Randy. "I think we may need to give you a refresher on what items can be monitored, Casey. You can be tracked if you use one of those things. Which is great if you're flying to the beach for lunch and you get lost, or get into some kind of trouble. But when you're trying to escape capture, it's usually best not to."

"Condescending jerk," she replied mildly, finding it hard to get upset with him, since he'd brought her to this heavenly place. This was a dream. Out in the middle of nowhere, aircraft, a hidden home, and by the sounds of it, Randy was also running his own contracting firm. She wondered what kind of work they did. And if she could get in on it, assuming she was still alive in a month or so. She felt safe with these two men. And the warmth that feeling brought after the horror of the past few days was so, so welcome. Maybe she could just stay there forever. She was pretty sure she wouldn't get killed if she stayed right there.

She pondered that thought for a second. It actually didn't scare her anymore. Being around Cameron, and Randy, she realized how much she had forgotten about being a band of brothers. About being with people who would stand with you no matter what. She'd lost that when she'd left the military, and being here, with Randy, who Cameron said he hadn't seen for over ten years, offering them everything without a second thought. Why had she left? If she'd stayed, none of this would have happened.

She looked at Cameron and Randy, pouring over the huge maps, deciding the three best places to refuel. Cameron's dark sandy hair and insane five o'clock stubble looked so hot to her. She imagined that he'd looked like that when planning a spec ops mission overseas. Grizzled, hard, in-charge. Randy was really handsome, but in a very different, almost Hollywood way. She wondered why he hid out here. Who he looked to for company. Or even if he did.

"There are quarters at the far end of the hangar. You can stay here for the night, sleep in, practice flying the bird, and then go. You should probably leave around two a.m. That will maximize your nighttime flying into the dawn. You should get to Connecticut in the middle of commuter time, which should give you decent cover. After that, you're on your own," Randy said, sounding more like guy-in-charge than the southern good-time flyboy he'd been when they were shooting the shit over the table.

"Copy that," Cameron replied, his eyes still on the maps and the route they'd been plotting.

"Can I go take a shower? I still feel a little grimy from last night," she asked, wondering if Randy could also magic clothes for her.

"Sure. Head toward the back of the hangar, go through the white door—you can use anything you find in there. There are toiletries, and workout clothes for sure. One of my female employees may have left some clothes back there too," Randy said without looking up.

Cameron did though. His gaze caught hers for a long second. She couldn't help but flash him a raised eyebrow as she turned to go.

The perpetual anxiety and the stomach churning, which had been a constant companion since she'd witnessed the crash from in the control room, disappeared. She got the feeling that they knew as much as she did right now, without her having to explicitly tell them any of the secrets she'd been bound to keep.

She walked the length of the hangar with her sandals in her hand, her bare feet slapping on the floor. The aircraft looked as if they were fresh from the manufacturing line, but she could tell that they'd just been looked after really, really well. She couldn't wait to get in the pilot seat to see how that new-looking Hawker flew. Regardless of what Cameron said, she knew it was a bad idea for him to fly across the country without her taking over when he got tired.

She pushed through the white doors and found what amounted to a whole other living area. There were two long rooms full of bunk beds, enough for twenty people. Each dorm room had its own bathroom with a row of glass shower cubicles, and changing and toilet facilities on the other side of the room.

She closed the door and investigated the other rooms back there. A large, seemingly state-of-the-art kitchen stood open plan to a large wooden farmhouse table. She only assumed it was state-of-the-art because it was all shiny chrome and steel. She could barely boil an egg, so kitchens were something she'd never really paid attention to. Next door was a room with ceiling-to-floor computer screens, and next to that was a room with sofas and TVs. Before they left, she needed to use those computers.

She stood in the hallway, looking in, wondered who stayed here, and what they were like, what kind of work they did, and for whom. This was a whole different type of military contracting. In truth, she was already envisioning Randy as being in charge of something very like *The A-Team*. Maybe Cameron was interested in joining him. Which in turn made her feel a little less bad for leaving the military and joining TGO. Not much though.

The bathroom called to her. She found large towels in the metal cabinets that lined the wall and gratefully, oh so gratefully, stripped off her shorts, Vegas T-shirt, and bra. She closed the cubicle door and turned on the water. Instantly hot. Seriously, it was like a perfectly constructed nirvana for military people.

As she reached for the wall-mounted shampoo, she suddenly had a ridiculous feeling that maybe she had died at some time in the past couple of days. Maybe Cameron was an angel who had brought her here. To this chrome-colored, empty world, with everything in its place, perfectly chosen for someone like her. The slimy hotel and the men who had tried to run them off the road had been some kind of celestial test.

"Hey." Cameron's voice came from the doorway.

"Hey, yourself," she countered, suddenly still under the pouring water. And then she remembered their tryst on the side of the road, which didn't really feel terribly angelic. So it was reality.

"I was going to have a shower," he said, somewhat redundantly. "But the other showers are being used."

A smile twitched across her face, but she fixed her expression into a frown. She opened the cubical door a couple of inches, and peered around, looking at the other showers. "I don't think…" She stopped talking when her gaze settled on Cameron.

He was leaning against the doorjamb, arms folded in front of him, tan T-shirt stretched tight across his chest and biceps. She noticed his beard had grown beyond the stubble she'd clocked the night before. She felt like she was seeing him for the first time since she'd been back to Red Flag. Really seeing him. Holy shit, he was hot. So, so hot.

She swallowed. Yes. This was the man she'd craved in the wastelands of Afghanistan. The operator, the confident man with the swagger. The guy who flew into the worst places in the world, and did what his country asked of him. The one who looked out for her, even though she hadn't known it back then.

He held her gaze, and she opened the door a few more inches in a silent invitation. Still watching her, he advanced, pulling his T-shirt off without missing a stride. As he stopped to undo his pants, she retreated back into the shower's heat, suddenly nervous. Not nervous of him, but nervous of watching him and falling in love with him all over again.

Shit. She needed to keep this casual. She couldn't fall for him. She couldn't. There was no way she could deal with that complication, in addition to all the other shit that was going on. Like it or not, she'd already kept a secret plan in the very dark recesses of her mind that had her running. Running away from TGO, Cameron, the authorities, and the whole country. Only if everything truly went to shit, though. Casey was not going to add the complication of love into the mix. She was firmly nixing anything that might make her hesitate to run, if push came to shove. And she was scared it would.

"Hey, what's wrong?" he asked, suddenly standing in front of her, pulling her head up with a finger beneath her chin. She started, unclenching her fists, which had unconsciously tensed.

"What is it, Casey?" he repeated with a surprising degree of tenderness in his voice.

She took a breath, and smiled. "Just a momentary freak-out. Nothing serious."

He didn't look convinced, but his naked, oh-so-very-close proximity left her uninterested in convincing him. He towered above her, making her five-foot-seven self feel petite. His hands spread over her shoulders, stroking slowly down her arms, until he held her hands and brought them up to his chest.

He reached for the shampoo behind her and, carefully positioning her head under the water, proceeded to wash her hair. Casey's eyes widened as she willed Casey-from-before in Afghanistan to witness what was happening here in Nevada.

With her head back and eyes closed, she squeezed the bottle of shower gel. Instantly a strong mint smell wafted around the cubicle, filling it with a wonderfully fresh feeling. She inhaled and rubbed her hands together, before stroking the length of Cameron's torso. There was nothing about this that wasn't a sharp turn-on. She ran her fingers through the sandy hair on his chest, eyes still closed, relishing his hard muscles under her hands.

She swept her hands over his chest again and found his nipples hard. He groaned as she grazed her thumbs over them, and his dick moved against her. Not that he was terribly close to her—he was just that…gifted.

He rinsed the soap from her hair, and used the shower gel on her too, starting at the nape of her neck, and working his way down. When he reached her breasts, she gasped too. The mint gel tingled on her nipples. "You see?" his low voice rumbled.

Her head fell back as she felt her nipples harden with the mint sensation, and his fingers squeezing and stroking. She felt as if her head was going to explode. Damn if she didn't need him to feel the same. She grabbed more soap, and foamed it up, before wrapping her hand around his hard dick. She made a ring with her thumb and forefinger, stroking and swirling around its length, over and over, trying to remember how it felt when he was deep inside her.

Cameron's whole body became rigid under her assault. He stayed her hand. "I'm going to come if you don't stop," he said hoarsely.

"What would you like me to do, instead?" she virtually purred in response. Her breathing was heavy, and the steam from the shower was making her light-headed. Or maybe it was Cameron. Maybe she didn't care.

"I think you're very dirty," he said.

Casey was a second from being outraged, before she realized what he meant.

"Maybe you need to clean me?" she suggested, looking up into his dark eyes, and biting her lip suggestively.

He half-grinned, and shook his head. "Vixen," he said. "Stand there and behave."

"Yessir," she said, raising an eyebrow at him.

He took more minty gel and washed her with his hands, across her back, her shoulders, and then crouched to wash her legs. As he rose, he said "That's it. You're all clean."

*What?*

The expression on Casey's face was priceless, in many ways. But at his root, Cameron was just gratified that she obviously wanted him as much as he wanted her. Needed her.

He pushed her gently against the frosted glass wall of the shower. With no fucking around, he covered his fingers with the tingly, minty gel and slid them between her legs.

"Is that better?" he whispered.

She nodded, eyes closed, mouth slightly open.

He moved her legs apart with his knee and reached as far as he could. The pretense was that he was washing her, and he could feel the foam build as he used the flat of his hand against her.

She titled her hips, virtually offering herself to him, but instead he slipped his fingers against her ass, pausing for admittance, and then moving on fast. She gasped. Every sound she made pulled his whole body tighter and tighter. His dick was straining to get inside her, but there was no condom in the shower.

She was so soft and hot against his hand, his fingers slid from circling her ass, to her hot center, to her clit, and back again. When he'd laid her on the hood of the car, he'd prayed for more light, so he could see her better as he'd made her come. His prayer had been answered.

"Look at me," he growled.

She opened her eyes slowly, working to fix her focus on him. She looked drunk. Drunk on him. As her gaze met his, his stomach clenched and his dick strained. It was as if they were joined in a g-force dive together, propelled into each other's gravity. He never wanted to be out of her gravity.

His fingers flexed against her clit again and he claimed her wet mouth. His lips slicked over her skin, and his tongue forcefully took possession of hers. She moaned, and sucked him farther into her mouth. As he fooled with her, her hands found his dick.

Jesus. This was going to take a short fucking minute. He increased the pressure on her with his fingers and felt her muscled start to stiffen. Her hand stilled on him as she moaned, and he flickered the tip of his thumb across her clit, sliding one finger inside her. Instantly, his finger was clenched as she spasmed around him. Once, twice, and then she stilled. A second later her shoulders dropped and her chin flopped forward.

One fucking day, he'd be able to do this on a nice bed, and take his time with her. Find out exactly what made her tick. Find out…and then his thoughts of the future were overcome by a thick fog as she continued to stroke him.

She used more tingling gel and stroked not just his dick, but his balls, and ass too. Every nerve ending was standing up, begging for her attention. He felt a familiar heaviness in his balls. But then she sunk to her knees and slid him into her hot, hot mouth. She tongued the underside of his dick, and squeezed his balls, using one finger—or something—to stroke his ass. There was no fucking list of anything in the world that could have stopped him coming, and he did, jerking uncontrollably into her mouth.

It felt as if the ground had opened him up and encased him in cement. His limbs were heavy and useless.

He'd never in a million years figured that at his age, he hadn't already had the best sex of his life. But fuck, was he wrong. Casey was…he didn't finish the thought. Couldn't finish the thought. He was too worried which word his brain would choose for her.

He defied the condition of his body, and lifted her to her

feet. Her eyes were half closed. "I could sleep for three days," she said.

"I feel you." He reached behind them and switched off the shower.

"Ready?" He was about to wrap the towel that she'd slung over the side of the cubicle around her, but she walked straight out. Her lack of concern at being naked in front of him, made his heart pinch with...something.

She grabbed a couple of towels from the closet and brought one back to him. Her body was amazing. Full hips, small waist, slightly larger breasts than he'd ever imagined when he first knew her. She was like a work of art designed especially for him.

Shit. He had it bad.

# CHAPTER 11

Randy sat in the quiet of his quarters, his feet up on his pale gray sofa, some reports unopened on his lap. Something felt wrong. His gut was rarely mistaken. All he had to do was figure out what exactly was bothering him.

Without a doubt, people were looking for the two officers in his dorm area. Luckily all his employees were out on jobs.

He knew all about TGO—they were in the same industry as he was, and he'd made the mistake of going to one government conference a couple of year back when TGO lectured all the other contractors about how to correctly structure their business to avoid paying taxes. Then during happy hour, they sent their acquisitions people around buying drinks and offering partnerships and capital injections to those with specialties they needed.

Randy had been one of those. TGO had been looking at expanding their security into a sole entity—they said it was to allow for greater autonomy—but Randy saw it for what it was. TGO wanted a security department they could disavow if necessary.

Firstly they'd pissed him off with lectures about tax avoidance. Most of his friends were still in the military—and his tax dollars paid their wages. He wasn't about to incorporate offshore just to pay less than he should. He wanted to be able to look himself in the mirror and know that not only was he still being a patriotic American, but he also wasn't going to be a fall guy for a huge corporate entity.

He wondered how the retired major had got suckered in.

A small red light in the corner of the room flashed on. He slid his feet off the sofa and sat up, looking intently at it. It stared flashing, and he jumped up, hitting the remote for his surveillance screen.

Eight footage streams popped up on the large-screen TV. The cameras scanned the area slowly, intersecting at exactly the point they were supposed to. There was no activity in the grounds, no lights, no dust, no footprints, no vehicles.

The other option was worse. Something airborne had penetrated his radar boundary. Airborne was bad. Very fucking bad. Cameron had left his minivan outside the hangar. There was no time to move it, whatever was in his airspace would see the dust.

He ran downstairs into the hangar, grabbing a camo net that one of his employees had draped over the coatrack to dry out.

He opened the exterior door to the hangar and paused in the doorway to listen for the sound of anything in the still air. It was a small rotor…something. He paused. It sounded more like a hair dryer.

Fuck. It was a drone. His brain was obviously weighed down with the Jack Daniel's they'd drunk earlier. The drone was on his left, sweeping the area. He had no idea what it was looking for but could only think that it was Cameron and Casey. He sidled outside and threw the camo net over the minivan as best he could before easing back into the hangar.

The drone buzzed closer and closer. It swept down his makeshift landing strip, and then turned, and buzzed back up. Fuck. The drone was a military-spec, an extremely high-end one. He grabbed binoculars from the coatrack shelf and tracked it. The camera slowly rotating on its belly didn't worry him so much as the two weapons attached to either side.

Fuck. He shouldn't have covered the minivan. He should have let it be blown up and move on. If they spotted the cover-up attempt, they'd know that Casey and Cam had assistance. And that was bad.

There was no way it hadn't spotted the car. Shit. He ran back into the hangar, sprinted past the aircraft, and punched the door open to the dorm area. In the first dorm room, he found them on the bunks, Casey on the top bunk and Cam on the lower. They were asleep, but holding hands, Casey's hand dangling over the side, and Cameron was holding it from below.

He pulled his phone from his pocket and snapped a quick photo. It'd be a nice Christmas card pic for them. Then he slapped on the lights and shouted, "Incoming!"

Both of them awoke immediately. Cameron rolled off the bunk to the floor, and Casey did the same, but she had to throw herself down farther. Then they looked up from the ground and saw him.

"Drone. I fucked up. I covered your car. But the drone is high-tech military spec. No way it hasn't spotted your car under the camo netting."

Casey looked up. "I take it drones are unusual around here?"

"First one since I set up shop here. Get dressed." He ran out and into the briefing room. He had just switched on all the systems by the time the other two joined him.

"What am I looking at?" Cam asked, eyeing the screens.

"That's the drone." Randy had managed to isolate it and track it with a camera at the end of his airfield.

"Oh my God," Casey said, eyes glued to the screen. "That's a TGO Syntec 8000." She looked away, her brain seeming to be running at hundreds of miles an hour. Her head snapped up. "Do you have fireworks here? Flares even?"

It wasn't a stupid question. Every small airfield used fireworks to startle birds away from a departing aircraft. "I sure do."

"Any pretty ones?" she asked.

He was about to head back to the storage area, but her words stopped him. He didn't say anything, but just looked at Cameron for some indication that she may have lost her mind. Cameron shrugged.

"You pair of...I can't think of an adequate word for you. The TechGen-One Syntec 8000 is their total-package drone.

Weapons, cameras, and heat sensing—everything any law enforcement agency or military may need. The problem is…" She paused and frowned, then seemed to shake it off as she continued. "The problem is that there was a glitch with all the prototypes. They worked great. Really great. But they couldn't differentiate exploding fireworks from weapons fire. There was an awkward moment in a Utah testing ground when one fired upon a late Fourth of July party."

Randy didn't need to hear any more. He had flare guns, and probably some display fireworks in the consignment load he bought for the runway.

Casey clocked him leaving, but she couldn't look away from the drone that she'd started to sell to agencies around the country.

"Why did you hesitate back then? What were you thinking about?" Cameron asked, moving closer to her, and lowering his voice. "You said 'the problem is' and then trailed off."

Casey firmed her jaw because she had finally realized what was wrong with TGO. In that split second, she knew everything. She was sure she did. She thought she did. But even the suggestion of her theory meant that she was so complicit in it, she couldn't bring herself to think about it. But it was so awful, she couldn't keep her mouth shut. "I think all the products they are producing for the U.S. market are…faulty in some way. They all have a flaw you can take advantage of if you know about it."

Cameron remained silent. And then it dawned on her

what she'd done. She slapped her hand over her mouth. "I'm sorry. Fuck." Why had she told him that?

He definitely didn't look as concerned as he should have been. In fact he looked pretty relaxed. He shrugged and opened his mouth to say something. But before he could, the familiar sound of rounds hitting metal echoed through the building.

They hit the ground in concert. She rolled so her back was against one of the chairs, and when she looked up, Cameron was crouching under the table in front of the screens. He pointed upward. There were holes in the roof. What the hell kind of rounds had gone through the metal roof and through the ceiling blocks?

Fuck. Casey looked toward the door. "Where's Randy?"

They heard the drone. "It's making circles around the target. As soon as the sound of the rotor fades, we'll make a run for it," she said.

"Copy that," Cameron said.

She concentrated on the noise the drone made. How many times had she been out on the test range listening to the same noise. She'd been exhilarated to be there, to be helping them fine-tune the accuracy of the weaponry. She remembered how excited she was that a fleet of these drones would take the place of actual soldiers putting their lives on the line.

Now, not so much.

"Go!" Cameron yelled as he sprinted to the door.

Casey scrambled to her feet and followed him. It was a crap shoot really, they had no idea which part of Randy's home and work space was actually the safest, but they did know that they had to get to Randy.

"I'm here," Randy shouted as soon as they busted through the swing doors. "Just sittin' like a coonhound in a hole."

"I have no idea what that means," Casey shouted back.

"I'm fine. They just got me pinned down a little. They're strafing the sides and roof of the hangar with armor-piercing rounds," he replied.

"Why didn't you just say that?" she grumbled.

"I've got the pretty fireworks you asked for, and also six loaded flare guns. So, what's your idea?"

They followed his voice and found him, hunkered down in the corridor leading to the dorm rooms. He had a GI backpack in his lap.

"I don't really have a plan. The drone is confused by fireworks. Anything bright that moves like a bullet or projectile. Its sensors should pick it up, move the drone into position to fire, and it'll fire at each flare, and then its source. A flare gun is okay, but pretty fireworks are better, because it'll run out of ammo faster."

"I've got to bring down that drone, or my planes will be Swiss cheese. I need to protect my babies," Randy said.

Cameron stood up. "Okay. We're going to run the drone dry of ammo, and then shoot it down. But, then they will know we're here, and they will send all their resources back here. So you've got to get out of here too. I'm really sorry about this. I promise we'll make it up to you."

Randy said nothing, just nodded and pulled out an old-style flip phone. He hit one button and waited.

"Hey, Jack. It's me. I have friends here, and we've been made in a big way. I need you to get here as fast as you can, and get as much stuff away from here as possible. I'm guessing we have about a couple of hours before they show up."

Casey could just hear someone replying "copy that" before Randy hung up. She remembered what it was to accept a mission with a "copy that" and not need to ask for further details. Maybe that was why TGO had been so anxious to hire her. Truth was, she'd never really known what got her here. The only thing that was important now, was taking them down, or die trying.

"Change of plan. You're going to fly the Hawker, and I'm going to take the Caravan. Jack can tow everything else away, no problem. Let's get that fucking drone," Randy said.

"I've got your six, Chief," Cameron said, then turned back to Casey. "You coming to see the fun?"

Casey didn't want to, but she was going to anyway. No way she wasn't going to be present at any fight that included TGO and its malevolent hardware.

They exited the hangar from the back, which for all intents and purposes, looked as if no one had been there for decades. The door opened soundlessly, but it actually looked as if it had been rusted shut forever. There were old farming implements strewn across the sparse grass. None of them looked as if they'd been used in the past century. She had to hand it to Randy—he knew how to camouflage his hideout.

He passed out guns to Cameron and Casey after he'd closed the door. They stood with their back to the corrugated metal wall. Randy rearranged the array of fireworks he was holding in his arms.

"Okay. I'm going to take these babies to the eastern end of the airstrip. Once I have that fucker's attention, you shoot it down from behind. Don't let it see ya, though. Oh, that reminds me. I took a super-cute photo of you two sleeping together. Do you want to see?" he asked earnestly.

Casey and Cameron looked at one another for an instant and then turned back to Randy. She glared at him.

"Alrighty, maybe another time." He winked at her and sidled around the other corner of the hangar.

She shook her head. "I can't even..."

"Let me tell you—being deployed with him one time was about the only thing that kept me sane. He was a spec ops JTAC. On most days he was the only thing between the SF team and certain death. And he was like this every day. So, don't think he's not taking this seriously. This is how I know he's in the zone." Cameron crouched with one hand on the ground, and took a fast look around the corner.

Casey followed suit. She was beginning to wish she'd deployed with Randy. She'd fisted her hands at the talk of being deployed. Her memories had been dragged to the surface in the car, and now it felt as if they were right on the surface, scratching away at her confidence, her nerve, her everyday thoughts.

She needed to shake that shit off. She prepped the rifle Randy had pressed into her hands. It had been a while. Taking a couple of deep breaths, she loaded a magazine and chambered the first round. "Look. If it's right here, I can probably hit it, but I'm not a sniper, and the last time I held a rifle was when I last qualified nearly three years ago."

Cameron turned around and grinned. "We're not on the range now, Casey. You don't have to take one shot at a time. Stick that AK-47 on fully automatic and strafe the fucker. Look." He nodded to a canvas bag that Randy had dropped at his feet before he headed off. It was full of mags. "We're not going to run out. Not before we bring that sucker down."

Casey looked at the gun in her hands. Yeah. She wasn't in the military anymore. She didn't have to abide by range rules. She didn't have to account for every round she shot at the drone. And no one was going to grade her on her accuracy. He had a point.

She swapped out the mag for a cartridge belt and locked and loaded.

At the sound of the first batch of fireworks going off, Cameron and Casey came out from the side of the hangar and watched as the drone flew full speed to the fireworks. It started shooting at the faint lights, and then aimed at the ground, looking for Randy. Cameron opened fire on it as it faced away from them.

Casey planted her feet wide apart, and held the gun up to her shoulder and did the same. The vibration of the gun against her reminded her more of the life she'd once had. The life before TGO. It was confusing. She'd experienced the worst and the best as active duty, and it was hard to try to forget bad things without the good things disappearing too. But as adrenaline pumped through her, she wanted nothing more than to get that drone on the ground and rip it to pieces with her own bare hands.

As it turned out, Cameron was far more accurate than Casey was. He was clearly still used to firing an automatic weapon. His rounds struck it a couple of times, and then it turned toward them.

Randy shot off a few more fireworks, but it barely registered.

Casey met Cameron's eyes. "Shit."

"Why isn't it going after the fireworks?" Cameron asked, ramming another mag into his weapon.

The user specs cycled through her brain as she filtered out everything extraneous. "It can be remotely operated," she shouted through the noise of the fireworks. "It's built to be autonomous, but it can be taken over by a user. Shit."

"I think it knows we're here," Cameron shouted back.

"No kidding," she replied eyeing the thing as it started toward them. "Look. There's only one thing to do. I'm going to run back there." She pointed diagonally away from the corner of the hangar. "And it's going to fly right past you." It was really their only hope. There was no way she was accurate enough to kill it if it were chasing Cameron.

He hesitated a second but clearly realized what she had. "Okay. Bring him past me."

She nodded. "Try not to get me killed."

"Sure, I mean, I guess," Cameron replied as if he were distracted. She had a feeling that he was in the zone too.

He hit the deck and lay in the long tufts of grass. He started drawing an arc in the air with the gun's muzzle, back and forth, back and forth. When he stopped at one end of the arc, she knew he was ready.

She took a breath and bolted out from the hangar. She ran back and to the left, ensuring that for the drone to get her it would have to fly right past the corner where Cameron lay.

As she ran, the sound of the drone got closer and closer. She visualized the operator getting her in his sites. Trying to find the sweet spot. Maybe someone was shouting at him to kill her. Maybe he just liked killing all by himself. How many of her coworkers would have been okay with killing a fellow employee? Jesus. Concentrate. Her running had slowed along with her thoughts.

Cameron unleashed a volley of rounds at the drone, and its motor stuttered. She stopped and turned around, only realizing her mistake a split second later. It was mortally wounded but still alive enough to take a few more shots at her. She dived to the ground, but it was too late.

Heat burned through her arm and leg.

# CHAPTER 12

Finish her. Finish her!" Grove ground out to the drone operator. The boy shook but hesitated before pressing back on the trigger. As he did, the screen went black.

Grove punched the young man in the head, hard. They'd tried everything. Bringing them in as experienced soldiers, bringing them in as inexperienced kids, and they always hesitated. Always fucking questioned orders. He was done with it.

"Get the fuck out of here, and don't let me see you again. Ever!" he shouted at the cowering boy.

He couldn't remember exactly where they'd sourced him from, probably one of the high school dropouts. Another one for the failed-experiment file. *Come on in! Work for us. Play computer games, but also get paid for it!*

Grove shook his head, but an idea flashed into his mind. Maybe they could reconfigure the drone footage so that it looked like a video game. Maybe they could give the drone operators missions, but only tell them that they were exercises. If they never divulged the active mission, they'd always think that they were just practicing. He smiled to himself, and made a note to mention it to Malcolm, one of the developers. No sense bringing it to Danvers unless he knew they could actually pull it off.

Meanwhile, he was stuck with Casey Jacobs. She'd been hit several times, by the look of it. So even if she wasn't killed, she would be slow now. Very slow.

He sent a message to Security Control to put a watch out on local hospitals, and for a team to get to that abandoned airstrip to see if they could trap them there and dispose of them. He looked forward to seeing the news of their deaths on CNN.

He cracked his knuckles. Danvers had Colonel Janke on payroll, and he was supposed to be taking care of a loose end on Nellis. Then there were his lose ends to track. He didn't trust Janke. Fuck. He was spreading himself too thin to be effective, but he couldn't admit that to Danvers.

He used the intercom to call into the main ops room. "Richards. In here."

Tex Richards was the only person he truly trusted to neutralize Casey Jacobs and Colonel Cameron. He was nicknamed the Terminator by his team because he just kept going, no matter how long or hard the job. That was the kind of operative he needed for loose ends.

Almost immediately Richards opened the door of the drone warfare room. "I have a job for you. A don't-come-back-until-it's-done job."

"Yessir," he replied, taking two steps farther into the room, his face blank.

Grove replayed the footage of Casey turning toward the drone, and her body jerking as rounds hit her. He paused it. "She's not alone. She's with a Special Operations dick, and probably someone else. They didn't end up in the desert there by accident. I want her dead, as well as anyone working with her. I don't want any loose ends. I want you to find out who she's spoken to, anyone who she could have confided in, and get rid of them. Make it look random."

Richards gave a glimmer of a smile. "Yessir."

Grove liked that he didn't ask questions, didn't hesitate. "Take a team. No more than three. No combat gear. Consider yourselves undercover." The last thing Grove wanted was to draw attention to the fact that they were working for what amounted to a paramilitary organization. The team had made a mistake in the parking lot, trying to take Casey Jacobs. They all wore their covert combat gear. Which wasn't so fucking covert in the middle of Vegas. Fucking idiots.

He needed some downtime so he could train the monkeys better. He'd put together the security group for Danvers, but hadn't really tested them until now. And they were coming up short all over the fucking place.

The Terminator would fix all that.

Cameron had seen Casey jerk as the rounds had hit her, and as he ran to her, he blamed himself. His focus should have been on the drone. If he hadn't flashed a glance at her, maybe he could have shot the drone down before it had shot her.

He skidded to his knees next to her. "Casey. Can you hear me?" He tore off his sweatshirt and stuffed it under her head. Her left arm and left leg were bleeding.

"Of course I can. I wasn't shot in my ears," she replied, gasping for breath.

He lifted her T-shirt in a rush of panic. He ran his hands over her belly, breasts, and shoulders, making sure there weren't any wounds other than the ones that were obvious. And the ones that were obvious weren't pretty.

"Why did you slow down?" he asked, and then cursed himself for blaming her for the devastation and impotence flooding through him.

She ignored him though. "Did you get it?" she asked through shallow pants.

He frowned. "Yeah, I got it. It's on the ground. Dead. I totally killed it." And now he was rambling.

"Make sure you get it—every bit. It's evidence," she said.

How in the world is she processing everything after she'd been shot? "I'll come back for it, after I get you inside," he said, crouching deep beside her. He pulled her uninjured arm so she was sitting up, then hefted her across one shoulder and stood.

She groaned loudly, as if between gritted teeth. "Nope that's not going to…" Her voice trailed off.

"Casey?" he asked, steadying her legs across his chest.

There was no response. The silence propelled him into hyperdrive. He ran with her back to the hangar. Randy was waiting for him.

"In here," he said, leading Cameron back into the dorms.

At the very end of the corridor, he pushed through a swing door. It seemed to be a fully equipped operating room.

Cameron hesitated in the doorway. "Dude, just tell me you're not doing anything bad here. I've only seen setups like this in movies when some bad guys implant shit in people, or worse."

Randy was at a loss for words for the first time since Cameron had met him. His mouth fell open, and then he frowned, injured. "I have three medics on my team. I promised them state-of-the-art equipment. We just never had to use it before."

Cameron looked around. Indeed, a bunch of stuff still had blue plastic wrapped around them.

"Yeah, okay, Sorry. I had to ask." As he said the words, he didn't even know why he had wondered about Randy. Must be the abject anxiety running through him. "Where…?" he asked, carefully shifting Casey on his hip.

"Oh shit. Here. Here." Randy ran to the wall and pulled out a large patient-examination table.

Cameron laid her down, and stood back. "I guess Jack isn't a medic?" he asked, stretching and clenching his hands in front of him.

"'Fraid not. This is all on us."

"All right. Let's get on it."

Randy started opening drawers and putting handfuls of instruments on a small metal table on wheels. He rolled it over to Cameron.

Cameron grabbed the scissors and cut off Casey's sleeve, and her pants.

Randy picked up her arm and peered behind. "It's a through and through. Let me check the leg." He repeated the procedure and gave a thumbs-up. "I think all we need to do is stitch here, no fishing. It's torn the skin, but only really grazed it."

Cameron breathed a sigh of relief. "Do you have any local anesthetic?" he asked, not wanting to work on her if there was a chance of her regaining consciousness while they were stapling her.

He fished behind him and picked up what felt like the stapler. He looked at what he'd picked up. "You thought we might need a speculum?" he asked.

Randy rolled his eyes and handed him the loaded stapler, and a single dose anesthetic. "Let's be quick. I don't want to have to drug her or do anything that might cause complications."

Cameron concurred. He stuck her with the auto-injector and then after a few seconds stapled both sides of her arm.

Randy took the stapler as Cameron passed it back to him. "I don't think I'll need it here. It's really just a flesh wound. It's going to hurt, but it's not that bad. I'm going to put some butterfly bandages on and see if that holds."

Cameron didn't reply. He couldn't take his eyes off her pale face. Honest to God, she looked dead, and even though he knew she wasn't, it scared the shit out of him.

"I'm going to make a call," Randy said. "See if one of my guys can give us more information."

Cameron nodded. "Ask about antibiotics. I suspect we should give her some."

When he left, Cameron drew a chair over to the table, and sat next to her. After a second of staring at her, willing her to wake up, but not really knowing if that was the best thing for her, he took her hand.

His whole career, he'd only had to deal with one gunshot wound. But even then he was able to pass him off to a trained medic after doing triage.

Casey whispered something and he jumped up and leaned in. "What did you say?"

"I can't move my hand," she half-whispered, half-choked.

He looked down at her hands and snatched his own hand away from hers. "Better?"

"No." Her eyes fluttered open, and as her gaze settled on his, she smiled.

His heart pumped out relief and happiness and…something else that warmed his whole body. Even his soul. *He had a soul?* He took a deep breath of relief.

"You passed out," he said in a low voice.

"I know. I'm a big wuss aren't I?"

"The biggest. A mere two bullet holes and you were out for the count."

"How will I ever live it down?" she said with a smile. She closed her eyes for a second, took a breath and sat up.

Cameron jumped up alarmed. "You should lie down."

Her eyes widened as her blood loss hit her. "Wow. I'm woozy. I feel as if I've been drinking." She winced. "And that I've been shot."

"Randy's getting info from one of his medics. I think we should be giving you antibiotics."

She swallowed hard. "Seriously. We should go. You have no idea how quickly TGO can mobilize. If I need meds, I'll take them once we're airborne."

She was right. He knew she was right, so he wasn't going to waste time arguing. But he was going to offer her an out. "We still can turn ourselves in. Talk to people I know. We can get you proper treatment that way."

Her shoulders relaxed. "Oh, God. That's really nice of you. But there are too many questions I need answers to. Too many concerns about TGO and what they're doing to our military. Too many people who are dead or missing. If it doesn't end here, where does it stop?"

He knew she was right. He'd just been trying to give her a way out. A semblance of a life. He'd wondered if being shot was a wake-up call for her.

But apparently not. He wanted to squeeze her. To tell her how proud he was of her, but he didn't want to condescend to her, or make her feel like it was her job to make him proud. He just smiled and nodded. "Whatever you say."

Randy's voice came over some kind of intercom. "Kit up, airmen. It's time to roll."

Their eyes met in amusement. He offered his hand and she braced herself on it to jump down from the table. Cameron grabbed some extra bandages, antiseptic, and a handful of one-dose antibiotics.

They made their way slowly out into the main hangar. Somehow the whole of the side of the hangar had been slid up into the roof, and the two larger aircraft had already been pulled out.

"I wanted you to take the Hawker," Randy said. "But the tracking and instruments are too sophisticated. You won't be able to escape them in this unless we dissemble the transponder, and we don't have time. So, I'll take this and lead them around in circles until I need fuel. You take the Caravan. It's slower, but it also has nothing on it that can be tracked. It's registered to Logistic Medical, so if anyone asks, you're going to pick up a patient.

"If you stop at a small airport, with no commercial operations, chances are the staff will only handwrite your tail number down rather than enter it into a system. When you get to Connecticut, ask to borrow the crew car. These airports usually have a car for visiting crew to use to go grab lunch. Just take that sucker and I'll sort it out when we go get our aircraft back." He took a breath and handed Cameron a large black kit bag. "Everything you might need."

"Thanks, brother. I mean it." Cameron held out his hand. Randy clasped it before bringing him in for a back-thump hug.

"Get going. Just don't get in touch until it's all over." He laughed.

"Deal." Cameron didn't know how he'd be able to repay Randy for everything he'd done.

Casey went in for a longer, slightly less balanced hug. Randy squeezed his eyes shut as he hugged her back, as if he figured he wasn't going to see her again.

Casey turned back to Cameron. "I think, under the circumstances, that you can drive."

He laughed. The Caravan was the aircraft they'd all

learned to fly in when they joined the air force. Whereas the Hawker would have been new and exciting, the Caravan was old and boring. "Copy that."

He heaved Randy's black holdall onto his shoulder, threw it in the open door, and then helped Casey into the copilot's seat. "I can fly this myself, you know. If you want to relax, you can lie down back there." He nodded toward the rear of the plane, where there was room for at least eight people.

"Dude. If I'm not navigating, we'll end up at Fort Bragg again," she said, using her good arm to put her headphones on.

"Fair enough," he replied. "The maps are sticking out of the pocket there."

They did preflight checks on the way to the end of the runway. They didn't have time for proper checks. Randy let them take off first, as they would have to wait longer after the jet to take off to avoid the air displacement a Hawker left.

Randy pulled in behind them on the flight line.

It was now or never.

# CHAPTER 13

It took them nine hours to fly to Connecticut, including two stops for fuel. They'd kept radio transmissions to a minimum and avoided controlled air space. As they'd taken off and circled around the pattern to head north, they'd seen a vehicle steaming toward Randy's compound, kicking up dust as it went. They hoped it was Randy's guy Jack, and not TGO's first responders.

The sight of the truck heading toward the hangar filled Casey with dread. She heard Randy take off but couldn't actually see him. Radio silence meant they just had to hope he got away.

Casey had opened the bag that Randy had given them when they were refueling at one of the small airports that Randy had recommended.

It contained weapons, another set of clothes, phones, and two stacks of bank-banded fifty-dollar bills.

Everything except the lawyer, she'd told Cameron.

Her injuries had dulled to an ache, and she'd managed to walk without a limp to and from the bathroom at the airports. There was nothing like a woman with a limp to stick in someone's memory.

When they arrived in Connecticut, they took the crew car, as Randy had suggested, and drove, exhausted, to a bed-and-breakfast with a VACANCIES sign swinging in the wind. He'd hoped that they wouldn't ask for a credit card, and when the owner saw his handful of twenties, he didn't.

They slept hard, especially Casey. She'd awakened shivering in the night. Cameron had given her an antibiotic and Tylenol and she'd crashed, only waking as the sun rose.

Cameron wasn't in the room, but she had memories, or images, of being wrapped in his arms during the night. He'd held her tight, suppressing her shivers with his body warmth. She remembered his hot mouth on the back of her neck. The comforting words he whispered.

She stretched her arm as far as she could without the constant pain intensifying. Her aircraft had been shot at a lot. But not her personally.

Where was Cameron?

It struck her that the same time three days ago, she would have been convinced that he'd jacked it all in and just left her. But she had no fear of that now. None at all. The calm that she recognized seeped through the fear of being shot to death. Her anxiety in the pit of her stomach was still there, but it was couched in a plan, and the first inklings that they might just be able to get away with this. TGO was a day behind them.

She looked down at her wounds. The bandages were a little grimy, but she was reluctant to change them in case she dislodged something that would make her start bleeding. The status quo was her friend.

Weren't her wounds enough to prove that TGO was trying to kill her? Shouldn't she just go to the police right now, and tell them what had happened? She squeezed her eyes shut against the what-ifs that were banging around her brain. What if they didn't find the drone? What if the police didn't believe her? What if TGO bought local cops off? What if she was dismissed as a conspiracy theorist? What if they still believed she had something to do with the crash? She was 100 percent sure that TGO could manufacture some pretty damning evidence against her.

The door opened and her head snapped up. Cameron had mugs of coffee and a piece of scrap paper in his hand.

"The owner let me use his computer. I have an address for James Turner. Where he used to live anyway," he said, placing the steaming mugs on the bedside table.

Casey took a deep breath. "Thank you. I figure we can ask his neighbors—see if they remember anything. I meant to use Randy's computer to do some searching, but…you know, we had to run for it."

He sat beside her. "I just did. Turner claimed that he had found an error in the safety reporting of a piece of aircraft software. He'd thought it was a mistake until he realized that someone had manually altered all the results. He'd told his supervisor what he'd seen and was assured that someone would investigate it. Then there's a black hole of information, until he went to a journalist, and was sued for breach of contract. And then he'd died."

That was pretty much the information Malcolm had given her. "I wonder if it's worth trying to get our hands on the court records? It might give us the journalist's name, or something." She felt impotent. She was desperate to find a smoking gun, anything that would free her, and nail TGO. "I need to find something. Something tangible."

Cameron paused and then turned to her. He took her good hand in his. "It's out there. If there was nothing to find, they wouldn't have been trying to kill us. They would just discredit us as crazy, and let us be. There has to be something. And we'll find it."

"From your lips…" she replied, wanting to believe him. What could they find that would conclusively prove that they were responsible for crashes and a cover-up? Her brain started to click into gear. "They're trying to kill us."

"Uh, yeah. A few times." He sat on the bed next to her.

"No, I mean, why? Why the urgency? Why not manufacture evidence, have a court case, like they did with James Turner? It's got to be the contract they're signing in a couple of days. If we're dead, they can pin the blame directly on us. With us still in the wind, someone could ask questions…postpone the multibillion-dollar contract."

"Oh God. Please don't tell me we have two days to fix all this, and prevent TGO from grabbing a ten-year contract that could put many other military members from every NATO country at risk?" He spoke the words out loud, letting her know that he knew that it was exactly what they had to do.

She gave him a pained smile. "Sorry."

He just laughed wryly and shook his head. "Shower?" he asked.

She looked at her bandages and grinned. "I may need help."

An hour later they were on the road. The town where James had lived was close to I-95, with a fairly easy commute to the TGO research facility outside New Canaan. They took the Merritt Parkway, which was marginally better than I-95 during the rush hour.

"I hope there's someone at home who can at least tell us a bit about him. I guess we should have gone last night when everyone would be home," she said.

"If no one's around, we'll come back later." He put his hand on her knee, reassuring her, and making her realize that she didn't think she could ever be in a car with him again without thinking of the first night they'd been in a car together.

They parked in the lot of a big apartment complex. There was a sales office with large pillars in front of it, and on either side were white town houses and apartments, with balconies and numbered parking spaces.

The got out and walked halfway around to the right, past a swimming pool, to the parking spot with James's apartment number on it. It was empty, but there was a shiny Mustang in the spot next to it. They looked at each other. "I guess it's Mr. Mustang then?"

They went up one flight of wooden steps and knocked on the door opposite James's apartment.

"Coming," a voice shouted.

At least someone was in.

A young man in his midtwenties opened the door. Music and scented smoke wafted out behind him. He coughed and grinned, wrinkling his nose. "You're not the police are you?"

Cameron smiled back. "We are definitely not the police. Don't worry. We just wanted to ask you about your old neighbor, James Turner. Do you remember him?"

The man's eyes flickered toward the stairs. "Yeah, I do. That was sad, man."

"Were you friends?" Casey asked, wondering if James was into pot as heavily as this guy.

"No. I mean, I we exchanged greetings. Held delivery packages for each other occasionally. You know, Amazon, etcetera, etcetera," he said quickly.

There was something not quite right about him, but Casey couldn't put her finger on it. He was describing a fairly common neighborly relationship—one that she herself had with Mrs. Wenders across the hall from her apartment—but he was being decidedly shifty. Maybe because he was high at nine o'clock in the morning?

Cameron asked a couple more questions as Casey looked into the apartment. He had a De Rosa bicycle in the hallway, and she could see a large TV in the back room, which was paused on a freeze-frame of some multiplayer online game.

"What do you do?" Casey asked with a smile.

"I used to work in a FedEx warehouse in Darien, but they

laid off a bunch of people last year…" he said, with one hand on the door. He was slowly closing it, and Casey wasn't even sure if he realized he was doing it.

"Okay, thanks for your help," Cameron said calmly.

"No prob." The door closed quietly.

Casey puffed out her cheeks, and expelled the air slowly. She walked to the little stairway and looked out at the swimming pool. "What now? Shall we just knock on some other doors?"

Cameron was silent. She looked over her shoulder and saw him pointing at the James's apartment door. There was a little mailbox to the right, with its lever up. There were two letters ready to be picked up by the mailman. One was a handwritten envelope addressed to someone in California, and the other was a misdirected letter. It was originally addressed to Mr. Turner, but the new occupant of the apartment had crossed the address out, and put *Mrs. Turner* and an address in New Canaan on it.

He slapped it on his hand. "This must be his mother's address. The online article I read this morning said his mother—a widow—lives in New Canaan."

"Let's go. I was getting a bad vibe from his neighbor anyway. He's unemployed and is smoking weed in the morning, and has an apartment full of fairly expensive things. He just struck me wrong."

He handed Casey the readdressed letter when they got in the car. It was a fairly short ride to New Canaan, and as it was a small town, finding the house didn't take too long either.

She looked at the letter. "Yup. 3145. Right here. The one

with the...you've driven right past it!" She shook her head in exasperation.

"You never park in front of your target." He looked at her as if she'd lost her mind.

"Dude. Not a special operator. That's you. I'm just a run-of-the-mill jockey." She undid her seat belt. "Besides, she's a woman with a dead son. Not exactly a target." So it bore repeating. "Do not go in there guns blazing. Do not interrogate her as if she's a suspect, and do not scare her with your tall, hard body and your brooding good looks."

He actually chuckled, and the sound made her feel fine.

"Let me do the talking," she said as they walked up to the ranch-style house with the pretty yard. Someone had spent a lot of time making it look amazing. She wondered if it was therapeutic for a woman who had lost her son. She hoped so.

Cameron stood at her back, looking up and down the street because he just couldn't help himself, and she knocked at the door, standing back so Mrs. Turner would be able to have a good look at them through the spy hole.

She heard scratches at the door, as if she were taking off a security chain. She wanted to exchange a look with Cameron, but she knew he'd clocked the noise too. In a beautiful, quiet, and, if she were honest, pretty fancy neighborhood, she wouldn't have imagined the need to use a security chain.

The door opened to show a fully-made-up woman of about seventy. She wore golf slacks and a golf shirt, and behind her was a set of clubs. It put a small chink in Casey's prejudgment of what she would look like.

Casey opened her mouth, but the woman cut her off. "I've already found the Lord, my vacuum works perfectly, and I do my own yard work."

Which left Casey at a bit of a loss. "Um, my name is Casey Jacobs, and this is…" She pointed behind her back. "Duke Cameron."

"Duke Cameron," Mrs. Turner repeated, a shocked look replacing the complacent one she'd had when she'd opened the door. She looked both of them up and down. "Casey Jacobs." Her mouth thinned in disgust. A thin finger poked toward Cameron. "You. You can come in. But she can sit her TGO ass down in the car you came in."

Casey felt numbness paralyze her own fingers. "You…you know us?" she stammered.

"You two have been all over the news. I've been watching. Ashley Banfield is my favorite. I have a Google Alert set up for TGO, too. I've been sitting in front of the television, watching the vice president of the United States praise the company that killed my son. Come in. Not you," she said, pointing at Casey, and then turning around and leading the way in. Casey was stunned on more than one level.

Cameron knocked her shoulder as he swept past her. "Come on," he said to Casey, nudging her inside before raising his voice so it reached Mrs. Turner. "Don't worry—I won't let her climb on the furniture or pee on the carpet."

"As if you could stop me," Casey murmured.

A *pffft* sound came from the front room.

Casey grimaced and closed the door behind her. Cameron was already seated in a rather old-fashioned living room, or parlor. The curtains were the same chintz fabric as the sofa and armchairs. He'd taken the sofa, and Mrs. James was sitting in one of the two armchairs.

She went to sit on the other armchair, but before her ass could touch the seat, Mrs. Turner piped up. "That's my son's chair." Casey jumped up, mortified, but caught the old lady looking at Cameron as if they were already conspiring against her.

He patted the sofa next to him. *Yeah, yeah, okay*. She sat and tried to reassert her position as the main interrogator. No not interrogator, interviewer. *Fuck*.

"I'm sorry to bother you at home, Mrs. Turner, but I'm in the same position your son was in. I'm desperate, and TGO's security has been tracking me all over the country."

"And now you've brought them here, to my house?" she asked tartly. Before Casey could backtrack and apologize, she continued. "Well, I suppose it wouldn't be the first time they've come here trying to intimidate me."

"Can you tell us what happened to your son?"

Mrs. Turner ignored her and turned her attention to Cam. "I heard on the news that you are a colonel in the United States Air Force, is that right?"

"Yes, ma'am," he replied simply. "Casey here, is also a retired major in the air force. We deployed a few times together—to Iraq and Afghanistan." Casey wanted to kiss him for underlining her credibility.

"Oh," she said, looking at Casey with a renewed interest. "My James always wanted to join the military, right from when he was sixteen. We couldn't understand why, no one

in my husband's, or my, family ever served, it was just something he was called to do." She paused and gazed unseeingly
at the hutch, which was adorned with plates, and photos,
and ornaments. "I never told him that his diabetes would
prevent his dream. I just thought he'd grow out of it." She
seemed to snap out of her reverie. "Tea?"

"Oh, um…" Casey looked at Cameron, who nodded
once. "Yes, please. That would be terrific."

Casey hung her head as soon as Mrs. Turner had disappeared into the kitchen. She was pretty sure she already
knew this story. He couldn't join the military, so instead he
joined a military contractor. And then he discovered something that wasn't quite right.

It was a sad story, but they really needed to get to the crux
of the matter.

When she returned with cups and saucers, and a teapot on
a brass tray, they allowed her a moment as she poured the tea
for all three of them, carefully using a tea strainer across each
cup. As soon as the ritual was complete, Mrs. Turner sat back
in her armchair.

"How long do you think we have?" she asked, before taking a sip of the hot brew.

Casey looked at Cameron again. She opened her mouth
to answer the question, but Cameron answered.

"I think we're about half a day ahead of them. Maybe less.
We flew here private, no records, but someone at TGO told
Casey about your son, so it's only a matter of time before
they figure it out. Do you have a safe place to go?"

She scoffed. "They can't hurt me any more than they already have. I'm not scared of them. Besides which, I have friends here to keep me company."

Casey frowned. Clearly she lived alone. What was she talking about?

She answered the unasked question. "I'm not crazy, dear. My friends are a twelve gauge in my bedroom, a .45 down the side of this chair, and another taped to underside of the shelf in the hallway. And one in the kitchen. They were my son's. He bought them a month before he was murdered."

There was a silent beat while Casey processed this gun-toting mother, and Cameron gave another of his low, rumbling chuckles.

"You say he was murdered, but the police report and the local newspapers say he killed himself. I didn't see any suggestion that he didn't," Casey said.

"Well of course not. I'm not stupid. I let the local police decide what it was plain they were going to decide anyway, and instead, I went to my senator—who I raised a lot of money for, incidentally.

"What did he say?"

"He told me that I should drop it. That I should grieve and put it behind me." She sniffed, less with emotion, and more with indignation.

"What made you think it was murder?"

"All the obvious things that the police overlooked. He'd bought a cooked, rotisserie chicken an hour before he 'killed himself.'" She put air quotes around the phrase. "He'd bought five new guns and spent hours at the shooting range to practice using them. And then 'killed himself' by hoisting a large rope—which he didn't own—around a rafter in his living room that stood twelve feet off the ground."

"Well, that seems difficult, but not—" Cameron started.

"The last medical problem he had, while TGO still gave him health insurance, was to repair a tear in his rotator cuff. He didn't have the range of movement required to be able to throw a heavy rope up that high. Or at all to be honest. He couldn't even help me take down my Christmas lights." She rolled her eyes, as if he were still in the room, and then her face crumpled slightly as if she was remembering, once again, that he wasn't.

Instinctively Casey got to her feet and perched on the arm of her chair, putting her arm around the old woman. Mrs. Turner let her for a few minutes, and then raised her head, sniffed, and declared that she was fine.

Cameron continued in a softer voice. "So you think the police deliberately covered it…"

"Oh my goodness, man. This town has a local sheriff who I used to teach in elementary school. He was a bully as a kid, and is a bully as a sheriff. Frankly you could fairly comprehensively bribe every person on that team with a rack of ribs and some warm french fries. He wasn't even worth talking to. I just nodded every time he declared something absurd about James and ignored him. That's why I went to my senator. I thought at least I'd have his ear, given the amount I raised for his campaign. All of the campaigns. Except this last one."

Casey's stomach started to churn. She had a feeling she knew where this was going. The phrase "Connecticut's favorite son" had been all over the last presidential election. "He's the vice president, isn't he?"

Cameron sat forward on the sofa. "Well that explains quite a lot. I wonder if TGO funded his campaign?"

Mrs. Turner gave him a "you tell me" look.

"Damn," Casey said on an exhale. She closed her eyes for a minute. It was too much. How could they fight someone that high up, with that many resources?

As if she read Casey's mind, Mrs. Turner gave her a nugget of hope. "There was one reporter who came around asking questions after James was murdered. I didn't dare say anything at the time—I was more scared than angry then—but she was the only person who asked the right questions. Her name was…her name was…wait a moment. She gave me a card."

She got up to rifle through the drawer in the hutch. "Here it is." She pushed her glasses up her nose. "Yes. Grace Grainger. She was the White House correspondent for *Vanity Fair*, of all things. Here you are."

She handed Casey the card. It was a plain white card with her name, email address, and the number of the WASHINGTON DC BUREAU on it. She pocketed it. Maybe, just maybe, they could get enough information to her for her to run it. Going public had to be their best defense.

They finished their tea and clarified a few points before heading back to the car. Casey was in her own world, thinking about Grace Grainger, and whether she would be interested in her story. Whether a true belief that TGO had killed James would release her from her nondisclosure contract. Whether between Mrs. Turner and Ms. Grainger—she may be able to get out of this and bring TGO down before they signed that damn contract.

# CHAPTER 14

Cameron didn't go straight back to the car. He hesitated in the doorway. Casey had already walked back and was already in the passenger seat. He watched her go, then turned back to Mrs. Turner.

"Don't hesitate to shoot anyone who comes in your door. Aim for the center of the chest. Even if they're wearing body armor, it'll still knock them down. Don't run into the house. Pick them off as they come through a doorway, whichever room you're in. But don't hesitate," he said, trying to convey the importance of his message with his expression.

She laid a hand delicately on his arm. "You're sweet to be worried. But I've been to the same practice range my son went to. And if anyone comes into my house uninvited, they're dead."

He nodded, knowing that a few rounds at a range were no substitute for the fear that would pump through her if people barged into her house. "Do you have extra ammo?"

"Of course." She started to smile.

"Are your safeties on or off?"

She raised her eyebrows slightly. "Off."

He grinned. "Good." At least she definitely wouldn't have to hesitate. He looked back toward Casey. "We'll call and let you know how we've done."

"She's like James, isn't she? She found something out about TGO?"

He found it interesting that she didn't question Casey herself about it when she had the chance. Maybe asking questions and having to show she had gaps in her knowledge was something she wasn't used to doing. "Yes," he said simply. "They've tried to kill her three times already. She was shot twice just last night." He looked back at Casey. "But she's still determined."

"Look after her," she said quietly.

"I intend to." He held out his hand, and she shook it, her grip reassuringly firm. She'd be fine with the stiff trigger of the .45.

Casey stood by the car with her hands on her hips. "What took you so long?"

"Just checking she knew how to shoot before TGO arrives," he said, getting into the car.

"You think they will?" she asked, biting her lip.

"I have no—" he began.

"Wait, she's running out," Casey said, putting a hand on his arm and making him feel things that he definitely didn't feel when Mrs. Turner had done the same thing. He shoved the car in park and jumped out of the car, but she was already knocking on Casey's window.

"I think you should have this. If TGO comes here and the worst happens, I don't want them to find it." She opened her hand and showed Casey a USB drive.

"What is it?" Casey asked.

"I don't know, but James had hidden it in a very dirty sock in the bottom of his laundry hamper. A place where only a mother would look."

"You didn't open it? See what was on it?" she asked, turning it over and over in her hand, as if by looking at it, she'd be able to tell what was on it.

"My dear, my son taught me all I need to know about computers: they can get you killed." She straightened, and waited by the curb as they pulled away. In his rearview mirror Cameron saw her retreat into her house.

As they rounded the corner, he looked out of the side window. Two black SUVs were pulling into the road at the other end. His pulse slowed, and his blood ran hot.

"What are you doing?" Casey asked.

"Look." He nodded toward the road, braking to give her the opportunity to see.

"Shit. Shit," she muttered under her breath. "No wonder James's neighbor had so many nice things. I'll bet they're paying him to alert them if anyone comes asking questions about James. Go around the block. We can…"

"…go in through the backyard. Yup. Already on it. You stay in the car, though."

"Are you fucking kidding me?" Casey said.

"You were shot yesterday," he said, pulling up outside a house on the parallel road to Mrs. Turner's. "Is this…"

"Yup. I've got a clear view of her house. We'll have to go over the fence."

"You mean *I* will go over the fence."

"Seriously, dude. If it was you who'd been shot, would you sit in the car while I went to the house?"

"Nope." Damn her.

"Then shut the fuck up."

*Goddamnit.* They didn't have time to argue. "Fine. Move fast." He jumped out, grabbing the holdall and slinging it over his back. She jumped out too, wincing, but not actually limping, when she walked. Hopefully the adrenaline would see her through.

As he approached the house, he felt different. This precise moment, as they walked around the hopefully deserted neighboring house and through to the yard, he felt like a jigsaw puzzle piece sliding finally into place. As if he were complete. This was what he trained for. This was what he had done for nearly twenty years. He was anxious for Mrs. Turner, but not in a visceral way. More of an intellectual concern. As if he'd been given this mission.

Fuck. This was what he was meant to do. Why had he ever traded it in for a life behind a desk? They crouched down at the fence, and Casey took a look into the house behind them. "Doesn't look like anyone's home."

"Good." He locked and loaded two handguns, and one rifle. He gave her one of the handguns, and she tucked it in her waistband. He held her back as she reached with her good arm to climb over the fence. "You know these people are after you? After us? When we go over the fence, we're basically presenting ourselves to them. If we don't make it, this whole thing goes down in flames."

"Service before self," she said, reciting a tenet of military leadership, her blue eyes shining with clarity, her face as open and uncynical as he'd ever seen it.

"Yup." He hid a grin. They were going to get this done. He had zero doubt.

They vaulted over the chest-high fence, and stood behind the garden shed that was at the bottom of Mrs. Turner's yard. As they acclimatized to the sounds, a doorbell rang clearly.

"I'm going in the back door. They will send people around the back here. Make sure they don't follow me in."

"Copy that," she said evenly, her eyes on the house.

*Bang!* A shotgun report echoed around the quiet neighborhood. Casey was scared, but calm. Her hands became suddenly sweaty and she swapped gun hands, to wipe them on her pants. *Get a grip, Casey. Remember your training.* Truth was, it was easier to stay calm when her aircraft was under fire. There were simply too many other things to think about to actually worry about dying. Here, not so much. But damn, she wasn't going to let Mrs. Turner be hurt anymore.

Cameron was already racing toward the small kitchen door at the rear of her house. She sidled around the wooden shed so that she was facing the house, and crouched, allow-ing herself a groan at the pain in her leg, since Cameron was out of earshot. More shots sounded. Dammit. The police would be here quickly. In this kind of neighborhood, they moved fast.

A man in black ran around the back of the house, gun up and ready to shoot. He didn't immediately see her crouching there, but when he did, he didn't hesitate to aim at her. She took the shot before he did. One shot to center mass. If he was wearing a bullet-proof vest, then he would be able get up again. But right then, he was on his back. That'd do, considering they really had to be out of here in fewer than five minutes.

She ran as fast as her bum leg would allow her to the side of the house where the man had come from, yanking his weapon from his unresponsive fingers and throwing it toward the rear fence. Two SUVs meant probably no more than eight in total—probably less.

There was a lock on the gate, so she engaged it, took a breath, and sneaked a look in the small kitchen window. She saw another man in black sweeping the kitchen, gun drawn. Okay then, she guessed she was going in. She checked her gun, even though she knew she'd only used one round. Five left. No room for error.

She entered the eerily quiet house. Shit. Her arm was shaking with the pain of holding it aloft in her firing position. Well, maybe she should make them come to her. The kitchen had a large center island, with copper saucepans hanging from the ceiling. She found a place to hide, and knocked her gun loudly against one of the pans. It banged into the one next to it, and then the one next to that, causing a ripple of clanging metal. She crouched.

She couldn't shoot him as he came in the door—first, she had to make sure it was a bad guy, and second, if she managed to drop him, she wanted him hidden from the doorway so that the next bad guy wouldn't see him.

A gun muzzle showed at the edge of the doorjamb. She ducked behind the counter, and moved to the far end of the island. Thank God for stainless steel appliances. His reflection in the dishwasher showed her which way to crawl around. She picked up her feet and slid on her knees.

When he was where she'd started, she jumped up and shot him. He didn't even have time to raise his gun. He dropped to the floor. Shit. She was good at this. Maybe she should have been a commando rather than a pilot.

She edged to the door. Okay, so this was one thing she'd been taught once about fifteen years previously: how to sweep a house. She'd pretty much forgotten everything she'd learned that week. Oh well, keep your back to the wall and hope for the best.

She slipped out into the hallway. There were three rooms—one to the left and two to the right. All the doors were shut tight, and she thought she remembered that doors are supposed to the shut after you clear them...or were they supposed to be open?

Shit. She inched down the hallway to the front door, which was chillingly ajar. She peeked outside. The SUVs were empty. She shut the door and locked it.

She heard noises upstairs. Stairs were basically a shooting

gallery. You were a target however you went up or down—there was no escape once you were on a stairwell, unless you jumped over the bannisters like Jason Bourne. No one actually did that.

She took a breath and took the first step. And then the second and third. The fourth creaked like a motherfucker, bringing a volley of shots from above her.

Without thinking, she pulled a Jason Bourne and threw herself over the shiny-white bannister, landing awkwardly on the carpeted floor, her gun skittering away from her.

Fuck. What just happened? She was pretty sure Jason Bourne never hurt his ankle, or let go of his gun.

There was one more shot above her, and then heavy footsteps on the stairs. She scrambled for her gun, gritting her teeth against the pain shooting through her whole body. All she could hear were steps coming closer and closer. Her foot refused to get purchase on the carpet and she was inches away from her weapon.

One last push and her other foot managed to anchor her against the wall. She shoved herself across the hall, and grabbed the gun by the muzzle, spinning onto her back. She'd pulled the trigger before she realized that it was Cameron at the bottom of the stairs.

She missed him by inches.

*Pilot. Not commando.*

His gaze followed its trajectory and its final resting place in the front door. "I'm never going to let you forget that," he said.

Relief flooded through her. She slumped. "What happened?"

"Mrs. Turner is the very devil with a gun. We have five operatives down. I'm a little hurt that they only sent five, to be honest." Cameron reached down to help her up. "Are you hurt?" he asked, concern etching his face.

"Just my ego. And my whole body jarred from avoiding being shot by you on the stairs."

"Not me. Him." He pointed at the man in black lying flat on the stairs.

Mrs. Turner tiptoed past him, as if he were detritus left from a party. "I have some lime in the shed," she said. "That disintegrates bodies doesn't it?"

Cameron laughed, and Casey's mouth just fell open. "Maybe just call the police?" he said. Then his face straightened. "No, wait. We need to think this through. We can't have been here, and all these guys, except one"—he nodded toward Mrs. Turner—"were shot with our guns. Okay, think."

Casey's brain started working again. "Swap guns. Wipe handles, and put Mrs. Turner's prints on them. We take the weapons you had in the house that you didn't use."

"That still means I have to deal with Chief Tiny Dick," Mrs. Turner said, the recent invasion of her house obviously affecting her language.

"No, no you don't. Look." Cameron pointed at the man on the stairs. "He has duct tape on his belt. We can call this a kidnapping attempt. You can call the FBI. Shit. Yes. Call the FBI right now, before the police get here. Tell them you just shot a kidnapper, give them your address, and put the phone down. They'll come fast. Can't imagine the local field office has many kidnappings in Connecticut."

"I can do that. But you had better go," she replied. "Go."

They nodded, and as they turned, the man who Casey had shot in the yard came barreling through the door with a knife in his hand.

Casey fumbled, trying to get her gun around in time. Cameron shoved her out of the way of the man's downward swoop with his knife. She bounced off a closed door and nearly bashed into both of them.

The man was huge. She hadn't realized when she'd shot him. He was at least half a foot taller than Cameron, and then she realized that Cameron had given all his guns to Mrs. Turner.

She looked at the stairs, and Mrs. Turner was pointing a gun at the men struggling for the knife. "No!" she shouted, worried that Cameron would get shot in the narrow hallway. The men struggled to get purchase on one another. The hallway was too small for the three of them to struggle.

With fear and adrenaline pumping around her body, she waited until the huge man was nearly on top of her, and she put her handgun's muzzle in his side, under his body armor, and fired.

His eyes widened, and his hand went to his side. He brought his bloody hand up close to his face. Red smeared across his cheek as he fell to the ground.

"Sorry, I thought I'd shot him outside," Casey said to

Cameron, who was blinking after being hit several times by the man one could only really call a steamroller.

"Well you shot him inside too." Cameron stopped and cocked his head. Sirens played in the distance.

He grabbed a couple of her unused weapons, and headed toward the back door. Casey watched him go, and then turned back. "Mrs. Turner, I'm so sorry we brought them to your house."

She pulled down her golf shirt a little, as if arranging herself properly. "I'm not. It's time this came out. Sunlight is the best disinfectant. And you can call me Biddy. Or Brigit, whichever you prefer, my dear."

Faraway sirens permeated the calm in the house. "I'll let you know how we get on, Biddy," she said, wrapping her arms around the older woman.

"I want to read about it in the papers too." She squeezed Casey back.

"Deal."

# CHAPTER 15

Casey struggled to get over the fence on the way back to the car, but she did pause to snag the weapon that she'd taken from the guy she'd shot twice. She recognized it as being one of TGO's prototypes.

She got over the fence and nearly collapsed at the bottom. Cameron ran back for her and lifted her effortlessly into his arms. "I can walk," she said as he strode to the car.

"Just saving you the trouble." He put her on the ground and opened the door for her.

She got in and slumped down into the seat, and closed her eyes. Cameron put everything in the trunk and they set off.

"I can't believe that even happened," she said wearily.

"I can't believe you shot at me either," he replied.

She didn't have the energy to object. They were a couple of blocks away by the time two patrol cars passed them, heading toward Biddy's house. "I feel bad leaving her to deal with the dead men in her house. And the chief," she said.

"I think she'll hold her own. The FBI will have a better idea of what went on. By the time they analyze the weapons and the house, hopefully everything will be out in the open."

"They better be. I promised her she'd read about TGO in the papers. Which reminds me. We need to see what's on this. It has to have the evidence we need," she said, holding up the USB thumb drive. She also pulled out Grace Grainger's business card. Maybe she could email her too. See what information she had. See if she was still interested in whatever she'd talked to James about.

"Get down!" Cameron shouted.

Casey instinctively ducked in her seat. "What is it?"

"Dammit. One of TGO's black SUVs is right behind us. I don't think they realize it's us though." He kept looking in his rearview mirror. "Damn."

The man driving the car had a large, bright red smudge of blood across his cheek. It was the guy they'd shot twice already. How was he still alive, let alone able to drive? The SUV swerved over the road, and went to overtake them.

Cameron reached for an imaginary phone and put it to his ear to block his face if the Energizer bunny happened to look to see who he was overtaking. He didn't. He was angrily shouting into his own phone. He overtook them, and then the car in front of them, and then turned off onto I-95 heading toward Darien.

"Damn," Cameron muttered.

"Can I come out now?" Casey asked.

"Yeah, yeah. He took the interstate, so I'm taking it in the opposite direction."

"I swear I shot him twice. I mean, Randy didn't give us blanks did he?" Casey frowned.

"From the look in his eyes, I'd say he was high on something. Speed? Maybe he had 'roid rage. Something is keeping him going. We've lost him now, anyway."

Casey was silent and started turning the USB drive in her hand. She turned it over and over, staring at it as if she could read what was on it.

He was concerned that she was staking everything on the thumb drive Biddy had given them. "You know, it could also be his Christmas card list," he said, trying to tamp down her excitement. He knew this was far from over. Besides, none of what James could have put on there would be pertinent to what had happened to the pilots on his watch. "I need more than whatever's on that thing," he said, nodding at her hand. "I need solid evidence if I stand any chance of getting justice for Major Daniels and Flight Lieutenant Dexter Stone. Which reminds me...I need to try get in contact with Captain Moss, my executive assistant. But I don't have any of her numbers, since I lost my phone." It had been a rookie mistake to put numbers into his phone without memorizing them. He'd never have done that eight years ago, but give him a few years flying a desk, and all his finer instincts were as dull as a mossy Gerber knife.

"So, let's find an Internet café, where I can check the USB key, and you can see if you can google her. She's probably on Facebook or Instagram. If you find her on one of the social media sites, you can message her," Casey said, a brightness in her voice he hadn't heard since they'd been in Afghanistan.

"Wow. Do you honestly think there is such a thing as an Internet café nowadays?"

She paused, and stared out the window. "Yeah, you're right. I don't remember seeing one in years. Okay. A hotel. A large hotel with a business center. They usually have computers so you can print out boarding passes, I think."

He acknowledged her quick thinking with a nod. "Greenwich?"

"Sure, why not. It must be fancy enough to have a decent-size hotel there."

He looked at the signs as they flashed by. Greenwich was forty miles south. "Where can I get the evidence that TGO caused the crash at Red Flag?" he asked baldly. He had to know if she would help him.

"In DC," she said equally as plainly. She didn't elaborate. After a few seconds, she added, "I think."

His hands flexed around the steering wheel until his knuckles went white.

As if she sensed his frustration, she started talking. "Look, I don't know for sure. The only thing that tipped me off were the threats I got after I floated the idea our product may have caused the crash. If they'd denied it and said nothing, I would have trusted them. But they didn't. The person I mentioned it to, sent me the information that led to James Turner. I took that as a threat."

"Or he could have been setting you up so that when you go public, you look like an idiot?" he asked. That was psyops 101. Convince someone that $X$ was true, and then show them how stupid they were to believe $X$, and watch them question everything they thought they believed."

"Do you think that's what they did? After our conversation with Mrs. Turner?" she asked, her mouth hanging rather adorably open.

"Do you? I'm not going to lie. All we have is a bad company, with bad employees. We have no proof of anything else yet."

She turned back to gaze out the side window, tapping the USB slowly on the door panel. Silence reigned in the car as they drove south toward Greenwich.

When Cameron wrapped his arm around her, and pulled her in close, nuzzling her ear, and being careful not to hurt her arm, something inside her melted. No matter that he was doing it so no one stopped them walking into the hotel. No matter that he let her go as soon as they were around the corner and heading toward the elevators.

"Conference rooms are downstairs. I bet that's where the business center is too," she said, pushing the button. Indeed, when they got in, there was a brass plaque on the wall telling them where the business center, gym, and ice machines were.

What the plaque hadn't said was that they needed a hotel room key card to get into the business center. Fuck. She peered through the frosted glass. There was someone in the room. "Go wait by the elevators, and then knock on the door once you know I'm in there."

He nodded and retreated. The blissful thing about having a special operator around was that they rarely needed explanations for anything. They didn't usually have time to do anything except give people room to work. What would it be like to have him around all the time? Her gaze followed him for a second longer than it should have, lingering on his long, muscular legs and the easy way he walked.

Casey smiled to herself as she turned back to the door. He walked as if he were wearing a flight suit. He was swaggering.

She knocked on the door. "Hello, can you help me? I left my key with my friend!" She made her voice slightly plaintive, and hopeful. Behind the frosted glass she could see someone swivel around in a desk chair.

"Please? I just need to print out my boarding card?"

The figure got up and walked to the door. It opened. "Thank you so—"

"I had to pause my game." It was a kid. Maybe twelve. Maybe younger.

"I'm sorry," she said, slipping through the door and forcing him back into the room. "What are you playing?"

He shrugged. "Nothing."

She smiled. Exactly the answer she would have given as a teenager. Her mother used to tell her that her whole vocabulary consisted of "no," "nothing," and "okaaaay."

The computer beckoned. She cracked her fingers and opened up a search engine. She should have shoved the damn USB drive in first, and seen what was on it, but first she wanted to see what CNN was saying about them.

The story had slipped to halfway down the page, and the only article right then was an opinion piece about the safety of running Red Flag given how many people die in training accidents.

That was good news, at least. People wouldn't be actively looking for them on the street the way she'd feared when their photos had been on TV.

She wanted to check her email and social media, but she just didn't dare log on and maybe give her location away.

Cameron knocked on the door, and she let him in.

The boy at the computer next door sighed heavily, as if Cameron's very presence was annoying. Casey twitched a smile.

"What does it say?" he asked.

"I haven't checked yet. I got as far as looking at CNN. Seems like there are more important things for them to be following right now."

"That's good to know."

He sat at the computer next to hers, and pulled up a Vegas news site that was more local to Nellis Air Force Base. While he read, she plugged in the thumb drive.

Pages and pages of documents and photos and whole files. It would take her days to get through it all. She was about to click the first doc, when she realized it would be more logical to order the files by date created, and read the oldest first.

"Kid. What do you know about Facebook?" Cameron asked the boy.

"It's an old people's sad place," he replied, eyes still glued to his screen.

"He's not wrong," Casey said, paging through a few more documents.

"Can you log me on?" Cameron asked. "I need to find someone."

The boy sighed. "That's not how it works. You have to set up your own account, then you can friend people." Then he muttered "lame" under his breath.

"I'll give you a hundred dollars if you can help me find someone and get a message to them." Cameron pushed his chair back so that the kid could see him.

"Show me the money first," he said.

Cameron whipped out one of the wads of cash Randy had left for them. "And that's just the start. I'll keep paying you, the more you help us."

There was one beat of silence, and then the kid paused his game again. Cameron stood and offered his chair to the boy, who sighed and muttered "lame" again. But Casey could see that he moved pretty damn fast into the chair.

"Who do you need to contact?" Casey asked.

"I don't think we should say in front of…what's your name?" he asked.

"Ben." Ben's hands started flying over the keyboard.

"It's okay. I think Ben's one of us. He might be a kid, but he's a gamer kid, and that makes him cool," Casey said, trying not to let a smile reach her face.

A blink-and-you'd-miss-it smile flashed over Ben's face.

Cameron rolled his eyes. "Captain Moss. Olivia. I need to get in contact with her."

Casey nodded and opened another file. It was a photo of a PreCall coding screen. She peered closer at the screen, and shook her head. She wasn't a coder, and she only recognized that it was the software because it said so at the top of the page.

She opened another file. It was the same picture. No, it wasn't. This had PreCall Russia at the top. James had handwritten an arrow at the side of a line of code. She brought both photos up. The line of code was definitely not the same.

"Can I get a message to my friend?" Cameron asked Ben.

"Not really. You have to be a friend, otherwise she might not ever find out you've messaged her. The best thing to do is to hack into one of her friend's pages and message her from that."

Both Casey and Cameron looked at him. "You can do that?" Cameron asked doubtfully.

"Sure. Well, nearly always, at least. Facebook is pretty easy, because it's mainly old people. Their passwords are easier to guess. First kid's name, or Password123. One time, my mum's friend's password was "six digits long" because she said the instructions said 'your password must be six digits long.'"

Casey's mouth dropped open, and Cameron snorted. "Mine isn't anything like that, by the way," she told them both with a meaningful look.

Ben snuffled a laugh, which Casey took as a win.

"That's my friend there." Cameron pointed at a woman with a gorgeous smile and blazing auburn hair.

Casey touched her own mussed-up hair self-consciously.

"See if you can find a friend I can pretend to be," Cameron said, placing another couple of fifty-dollar bills on the desk in front of him.

# CHAPTER 16

Animal strode along the corridor toward Commander Cameron's office. No one had been able to get in touch with him, but he figured his exec may be able to track him down and pass word that they'd found the pilots alive.

He stopped in the doorway when he saw—his eyes flashed down to her name tag—Captain Moss. Her long red hair was tied up in an utterly efficient thing on the back of her head, but little bits had floated out and were tucked behind her ears.

He wanted to run his hands through that hair. His fingers spread imagining the weight of the cool, shiny auburn hair.

He inhaled, as if he were able to smell the shampoo she used. And then he realized that she was looking at him with a frown on her face. "Is everything okay, sir?"

He snapped a salute, automatically, clearly without thinking. No one saluted indoors, and he was pretty sure he outranked her. But as his hand fell, she saluted back. He was totally charmed that she'd humor him, but he winced none the less.

"Don't worry, sir. Everyone gets flustered in this office." She bent back over her notebook as she finished writing.

He wanted to tell her that he was the best pilot on the airfield, that he didn't get flustered at anything, but his racing heart at the sight of her betrayed that thought. He cleared his throat. "We found them," he said in an inexplicably hoarse voice.

"You what? You found...Colonel Cameron?" She stood up eagerly.

"What? The colonel is missing?"

"Since last night." She bit her lip in an adorable way. "I can't tell you how unusual it is for him to be AWOL."

Animal was stunned out of his reverie. "That doesn't sound good." His mind raced. It was TGO. It had to be. Damn. "I need to find Casey Jacobs. She would be able to shed some light on this."

"She seems to be missing too. They went on a date last night, and never came back," Captain Moss said.

"Shit," he said under his breath. He was kind of happy for her—dating a real live man, instead of living for her flying career. But he'd lost track of her after she left the air force, so maybe she was a dating machine. He shrugged. "The commander? Is he decent?" He didn't know why he asked, but his friend obviously thought he was dating material. And he wanted to know if the woman he was going to marry—the one standing in front of him, whose first name he didn't even know yet—was working for a good guy.

"He's the best. That's why I'm worried about him being AWOL. Wait. Who did you find?"

"The missing pilots."

"Oh my God!" She slumped down in her chair as if her legs had refused to hold her.

He took a step forward, concerned. But she placed her head on the desk for a second, before raising it with a beautiful, heart-stopping smile. "That's the best news ever. I mean, *ever.*" Tears shone in her eyes, making her look like a freaking angel "How did you find them?" She took a couple of deep breaths. "I mean—are they okay? You found them…"

"Alive, yes." He tilted his hand in a so-so gesture. "Eleanor was in bad shape. She was medevacked to the hospital. Dexter Stone was dehydrated and had a really bad concussion, but he'll live. He's got a wicked hard head. They were attacked out there though. Eleanor was shot."

"TGO, right?" She rose from her desk and planted her fists down on her desk. Her face radiated fury.

He held his hands up, as if to ward off her anger. "I don't know. I…assume so."

"But the commander was with Casey Jacobs—that bitch. She must know what's going on here. She must be the reason he's missing."

He sat on the corner of her desk, the pull of being that little bit closer to her too much to fight. It was like she had her own gravity field and he didn't have the force to resist it. "I know Casey. We served together in Afghanistan. She's good. I swear it to you. She's the one who let us out of the base so we could go search for Eleanor and Dex. If she's missing, and your commander is missing, then something has happened to them both."

Moss went white. "This is worse than being at war. Down-range, you have a good idea who your enemy is. But this is worse. I don't know who I can trust. I don't know what to do about my missing boss. No one seems to know who's in charge now he can't be found. It's like someone knows exactly how to cripple us and leave us unable to fix anything."

"I don't think anyone planned this, but I know someone will take advantage of our weakness. Probably the best thing you could do to help is to do all you can to find the next ranking officer on base."

"I have. It's a long, disparate story of people being away from base, emergency leave, or people attending a school. But we have the commander of the neighboring base coming in today, although he's only been commanding that base since Tuesday. And the base is tiny. Like eighty people. It's not Nellis." She shrugged, seemingly unconvinced that the inbound commander would be able to do anything.

"Don't worry. We've found one set of missing people. I'm sure we'll find your boss."

"Will you come back and let me know if you hear anything?" she asked.

He noticed a sliver of fear in her expression. "Of course. Give me your phone number and I'll keep in touch the whole day." He was bad. But he wanted to be able to talk to her whenever he wanted.

"You'll come back to see me?" she asked.

"Try keeping me away," he blurted before he realized exactly what he'd just said. He looked down at his hands rather than see the shock on her face. What was wrong with him?

But by the time he'd stood up and risked a glance at her, she was smiling. "I wouldn't dream of it," she said.

"What? I mean…wouldn't dream of what?" he stammered, cursing himself for completely losing his normal and well-practiced swagger.

"I wouldn't dream of keeping you away," Captain Moss said, rising to meet him eye to eye.

In that moment, he would have traded every Olympic medal, every military medal, to sweep her into his arms and kiss her. But he didn't, of course. It would have been wildly inappropriate.

He took a step back and internally laughed at himself. Inappropriate was usually exactly where he lived. But not this time. Without him being entirely conscious of it, his brain had already put the brakes on his moves. Something inside told him that he should wait, take his time, get to know her before jumping her bones.

He cleared his throat and took another step away. "I'll bear that in mind, Captain Moss."

She said nothing as he turned to leave.

Olivia watched him leave her office, her head tilted in surprise. Animal was a legend. She never imagined she'd even get a chance to talk to him. To ask him about his missions and the crazy, brave stories she'd heard about him. How he saved lives and performed physics-defying maneuvers in the air. And there he was, promising to come back to talk to her.

She sighed and sat down again. He was crazy-handsome, with a glint in his eye that told her—and most likely everyone he ever spoke to—that he was thinking bad things. She'd really thought for a second that he liked her. And she'd basked in that feeling until he left.

But she also knew nearly every woman on base came away with similar stories of encounters with him. She would have totally jumped him given half the chance. And that wasn't cool at all. She'd never one-night-stood—standed? She frowned at the conundrum. God, she was so pathetic, she didn't even know what the term was. Anyway, she totally would have given up her one-night-stand cherry to him. Any day of the week.

She took a long, deep breath and again noticed the open door to Colonel Cameron's empty office. Her stomach clenched, and the acidic sensation in her sternum returned. There it was. Animal had made her forget for a second the deep anxiety she'd been internalizing since the morning.

She was reaching for her number two pencil, when something binged. What the hell? She spun slowly in her chair, examining all the devices in the office. It wasn't the printer, or the fax. It wasn't the DSN line, or the emergency phone. The bank of radios were all perfectly lined up on the charger, so it wasn't them. The tone sounded again.

It definitely came from her PC. She peered at the applications she had open. Was it Facebook? She never opened that at work. And then her gaze fell on her cell phone. Shit. She'd forgotten to leave it on the cell phone ledge outside in the corridor. Staff were forbidden from bringing anything with

Wi-Fi or Bluetooth into the offices where there were secure comms. She looked around as she grabbed the phone, more worried about anyone seeing her with a phone than about whoever was making her Facebook alert go off, and slid into the corridor so she could tuck her phone away on the ledge.

There was no one in sight, so she paused to look at her phone. Her sister was posting to her page. That was weird. Her sister rarely used Facebook. She was twenty-six and had four kids under the age of eight. She rarely had time for anything.

The message made no sense either. Maybe she'd been hacked?

CAME to see you, but you R ON leave. Only reply if you're alone.

She stared at the message next to the avatar picture of her sister and Olivia's nieces and nephews. *What the—?* She started to write back "Are you high?" when she understood. She looked around, as if anyone would judge her for being a slow num-nuts.

I'm alone. Was this really Colonel Cameron? Or was she being catfished?

I need your help. But you can't tell anyone. You can't trust anyone.

How about you? How do I know you are who you say you are?

?????

What do you say to me every morning? She wasn't going to be a sucker.

"Sit down, Captain." I also usually shake my head at the fact that no matter how many times I say it, it doesn't sink into your brain.

Well she asked for that, she supposed. She was also superpsyched that he was...well to be honest—still alive.

What's your phone number?

You've got my phone number. What's going on?

No. I don't. No one's been able to get hold of you since yesterday. Where is your phone?

In the baby's crib. Using it as a baby monitor for a sec.

Oh, dear Lord. Her sister had heard the Facebook alert, and had blithely jumped into the conversation. She scrolled up to see how long her sister had been chatting instead of the colonel.

Can you give me your phone number so I can contact you?

That was clearly the colonel.

What? I didn't write that? Liv. What's going on?

Sweet hell. She typed Cell: 910 555 4501 and then: Sis. I hear
Cody crying.

Really? BRB

She felt bad at taking advantage of her sister's baby-addled
mind, but she needed to get off Facebook. She closed the app
and waited for her phone to ring.

And waited. She leaned up against the wall, and waited
a little more. Why had she given him her cell phone number? She couldn't take her cell phone into the office with
her. Although, really—who was going to reprimand her?
There was no one here above the rank of Colonel
Cameron, and he'd clearly implied that he wanted to contact her.

She looked toward the door, wondering if she should
take a walk in the warmth of the afternoon sun. Maybe
she'd bump into the Animal again. Also—if she was going
to crush on him, she should probably find out his real
name.

Her phone vibrated in her hand and an unknown number
popped up on the screen. She stood at attention as she answered it.

"Captain Moss?" she said.

"Captain. It's good to hear your voice."

She slumped in relief. "And yours, sir. We thought…well we

thought you were dead. Or that your date went really well." She paused. "And some people think you're involved with the crash."

"Yeah, I got that from the TV. What's going on there?"

She shook herself. "Oh my God. Animal was just here. They found the pilots. The British one is injured, but okay. Major Daniels is in bad shape. She'd been shot."

"Presumably not by the British pilot?"

"No, sir. By persons unknown. We're sure it's TGO," she said quickly. "I have no proof, but I'm sure. They were the only people on the range at the time. The British pilot says he would recognize the person who did it if he saw him again."

"Casey was attacked in a parking lot after she let Animal out. I rescued her, and we've been on the run ever since," Cameron said. "We're looking for evidence."

"Look fast. Things are unraveling here with no commander," she said, her hand over her mouth so no one could hear her disrespect the chain of command. "Colonel Witten is on his way from Dyce. But he's only been a base commander there for three days. Sir. Things are going to shit here, if I may speak frankly."

"They found the pilots. Alive," Cameron told Casey, sure that the news would make her feel a whole lot better.

She slumped in the business center chair. "That's such a relief. Oh my God. That's everything. How are they? What did they say?" she said quickly.

"Major Daniels was shot by as yet unknown people." He

raised his eyebrow at her. "Flight Lieutenant Stone was injured and dehydrated, but rallied pretty quickly."

"Are you CIA or something?" the kid asked, looking interested for the first time.

Cameron had all but forgotten he was there. "Nothing like that. But we are on a mission."

"That might be cool," Ben conceded.

"Yeah, but you can't tell anyone," Cameron said, piling up a little stack of fifty-dollar bills next to his computer. "Deal?"

"Deal." Ben took the money and stuffed it in his pocket. He pulled a fake grin, and then went back to his game.

"To DC," Casey said as she stood up, nodding toward the door. She ejected the USB drive and said goodbye to Ben.

He grunted.

Casey raised her eyebrows, and nodded for Cameron to follow her out of the business center.

"I know what is up with TGO. I know what they're doing. And we need to get to DC as soon as we can."

Cameron took her elbow and led her back out to the car. "We better go fast. I didn't think about it before, but do you think they can track that you plugged in the USB drive here? Could it have triggered anything that would make them come for us?"

Casey's eyes said everything she needed to say.

"Fuck. Let's go." Cameron jumped in the car and peeled out of their parking place.

"TGO's Connecticut office is about twenty miles north of here. How long were we in the business center?" she asked.

"About fifteen minutes. We have five minutes on them at best."

Cameron hit the I-95 on ramp at seventy miles an hour.

# CHAPTER 17

The door to the business center burst open, slamming against the wall. Ben jumped and looked around, automatically pausing his game as he did.

A giant stood in the doorway. He was all in black, with guns everywhere and blood on his face. Ben suddenly needed the john real bad. Like, real bad.

"Where did they go?" the giant bellowed.

"Wh...who?" stammered Ben,

"The man and woman who were here twenty-two and a half minutes ago."

Ben looked back at his computer. The image on his screen was of a huge man in combat gear, with weapons all over him. He looked back at the man in the doorway. "Do you have the magic serum that blinds your foes?"

"Where did they go?" The man advanced into the room, and suddenly it seemed like the room was shrinking.

Ben wasn't about to lose a life over this. He was already

two lives down. "Give me three hundred dollars and I'll tell you."

The soldier picked him up off his seat. "Tell me."

"I...I only just got here," Ben gasped out. He remembered what that one guy had said about being on a mission. He didn't know who he was, but this was obviously the bad guy.

The huge soldier guy dropped him back into his seat, and stomped out of the small room.

Ben swallowed, and picked up his phone. "Mom. Can you bring some clean pants down to me?"

Malcom's phone rang and rang. Casey guessed he was looking at the unknown number and hesitating, as anyone does when a strange number popped up on caller ID. Then he answered.

"Hello?"

"Hi. This is Care-Bear from the dry cleaners at Fourteenth and K Streets. I'm just calling to tell you that your cleaning is ready. Can you come pick it up?" Casey winced as she spoke.

There was a long pause. Was he looking at the phone in puzzlement, or was he motioning to security to listen. "Sure. Sorry I left it so long, I'll be right there. Fourteenth and K you said?"

"Yes, that's right. I'll see you soon." She hung up, and looked at Cameron. It had been her idea. Malcom had called her Care-Bear once when they'd got drunk together. She'd made sure he'd never done it again.

They'd driven past her apartment, and Cameron had spotted two units of people watching the block. She hadn't seen them, but she trusted that they were there. The only option left to them was persuasion. But before they showed their hand, she had to figure out who's side Malcolm would fall on when the shit hit the fan.

"So, now we see if he reports me to TGO security, or if his warnings were genuine."

They were sitting on a bench in Franklin Square, drinking takeout coffee. Watching the building on the corner of Fourteenth and K Streets. Her hand was shaking, despite the weather being warm enough that she couldn't use it as an excuse. She wondered if she would ever stop shaking. Malcolm was their last chance to get their hands on the evidence she needed. Even then, she'd have to find a lawyer in the city who wasn't in some way connected to the White House, or to TGO.

If Malcolm turned up alone, then she could trust him. If he didn't, then it was pretty much all over and she'd have to find somewhere to hide while she tried to bring TGO down. Her eyes dropped as she thought it. Cameron would also have to hide. She had wrecked his life in three days.

"Is that him?" Cameron asked. Taking a sip and nodding toward a man with mop hair and wearing a bright orange sweater.

She really didn't even have to see his face to know it was him, but she waited to be sure. He turned around, looking at all the people passing him, and then into the window of the store that was actually at Fourteenth and K. It wasn't a cleaner.

There were no telltale black SUVs, no one looking like operatives, or security. And he didn't call anyone while he was waiting for her.

"Wait here," Cameron said, flipping up the hood on his sweatshirt. He walked along Fourteenth Street, looking at everyone who was hanging around in sight of Malcolm. Then he passed Casey's friend without looking at him, and watched the people coming and going along K Street.

He went back and sat down again.

"Well?"

"There's no one I can see that makes him look compromised. But there's one way to find out." A gaggle of college students was flocking toward the coffee shop halfway down the block. He went up to one of them and chatted to her out of Casey's earshot. Even though Casey couldn't hear what he was saying, she did clock the admiring looks the students were giving him. The kind of looks she'd be giving him if they weren't walking dead people.

Suddenly she saw him as she used to when they were in Afghanistan, and through the eyes of the lovely young women he was talking to. Wait, what? She watched as one of the girls slipped him a card. Students had business cards now?

They walked off again, and Cameron returned to her.

"You got lucky," she said, nodding toward the pocket where he'd stashed the card she'd given him.

"Watch." He motioned at the girls he'd been speaking to as they crossed the road. A woman with short dark hair approached Malcolm and asked him the time.

He checked his phone and told her. The woman lingered a couple of seconds, and then thanked him by putting a hand on his arm, and caught up with the others.

"What was that all about?"

"He's clean. I gave her a fifty to ask him the time, and make small talk for about ten seconds. I figured if anyone was watching him and saw him talking to a woman with dark hair like yours, they'd jump on her. But no one even twitched. I surmise that he didn't tell anyone he was meeting you."

"Nicely done. Let's go then, and I'll call him again in a few minutes and ask him to meet us tonight." She got up, but Cameron pulled her down again.

"Wait for him to leave, and don't look at him at all. Look over there. Watch the people come out of the movie theater. I'll tell you when he's gone."

She did as she was told. "Why are people in the movie theater in the middle of a workday?" she wondered. Their lives must be blissfully calm to be able to spend a few hours tucked away in the dark while everyone else was working. She was envious. After this past week, she wanted an ordinary life. She wanted to work at a movie theater and be able to just worry about paying her cable bill instead of worrying that a multinational corporation wanted her dead.

"He's gone. Let's go." Cameron took her hand in his,

and then pulled her closer, wrapping his arm around her. She nestled in the warm comfort of his body. Her heart rate settled as they walked toward the Washington Mall.

When they reached the green open space, she reached for her phone and pressed redial. This time he picked up right away. "Hello?"

"Can you talk?" she asked.

"Yes. I'm in a taxi. Are you all right? I...didn't know what to think."

"I need help. TGO tried to kill me." She held her left arm for a second. "In fact, they've already shot me twice. I just need you to do one thing for me. Can you help?"

There was a moment of silence that unnerved her. "Will it get me shot?" he asked.

"No. It's easy, I promise. I had a hard copy of the prototype manuals and logs for PreCall—the software that anticipates pilots—"

"I know what PreCall is," he said interrupted.

"I just need an electronic copy of the whole development file. If you could download it to an external drive and bring it to me, I'd owe you. I'd owe you everything." She'd ask him to email it to her, but that would put him firmly in TGO's crosshairs.

"Where shall I bring it?" he asked calmly.

"Our usual place. Tonight. Say eight p.m.?" she asked, searching Cameron's eyes for an acknowledgment.

Cameron nodded.

"I'll see you there. Hey, Casey. Be careful, okay?"

"I will." She choked back the desire to say "you too" because she didn't want to freak him out. She hung up.

"Here goes nothing," she said.

Casey and Cameron sat outside the bar in Alexandria. "Are you sure about this?" he asked, not taking his eyes off its entrance. Al Chile's definitely seemed to be a spot for locals rather than a destination for an evening out. Most of the patrons that he'd seen going in held briefcases, or came from neighboring buildings where they either worked or lived. A few just came out almost immediately with a brown paper bag for takeout.

Casey didn't answer. She just stared at the restaurant.

He grabbed her hand, and she spun around, startled. And then as her gaze met his, her face crumpled into insecurity. "No. I'm not sure about this. But this is all we have left. He passed the test this morning. That's more than we had before."

"Let me go in first," Cameron said. "I'll sit at the bar and keep my eyes on the door. When you come in—wait ten minutes or so—don't look at me, don't avoid me, just concentrate on getting a drink and finding a table where Malcolm can find you easily. We want this to go smoothly. As soon—"

"I know. As soon as I have it in my hands, go to the bathroom and head out the rear door and exit through the loading dock. I've got it." She knew her voice sounded slightly more irritated than she wanted, so she looked back at him. "Sorry."

He reached over to her and slipped his cool hand behind her sweaty neck. "If this goes bad, just try to get away. If they try to take you, and I can't stop them, then don't say anything to anyone. I will get to you. You understand?"

She nodded, although they both knew that the time for them trying to grab her was already over. They were going to silence her forever.

Casey sat at a booth in the corner. As soon as she sat down and ordered a beer, she realized she'd made a mistake. There was no way of getting out of a booth. With a table, she could run away. A booth held her captive. Her whole body went cold. She couldn't meet Cameron's eyes, but she knew he'd see her error too.

She took a breath and tried to concentrate on something else. A beautifully coiffed blonde entered the bar. She was definitely not a regular patron. She was dressed in a tight black evening dress, with a slit up the length of one long leg. She basically looked like a model. A completely out-of-place model or actress. Her features were fine, her chin held aloft.

Every eye in the place was on her, and she stopped in her tracks as she suddenly realized that she was the center of attention. After a couple of seconds, her chin lowered and she hiccoughed loudly. Then she took a step toward the bar, and stumbled a little. A man jumped up to steady her.

She put up her hand. "Eeem okay, darlink," she said in an unrecognizable foreign accent. She got to the bar and put her small evening bag on the bar, except she misjudged it and dropped it on the floor instead. Casey felt bad for her, and really wanted to get up and help her, all the while desperately wanting to exchange looks with Cameron. But as she stood, Malcolm entered the bar.

Casey's attention was immediately on him. She waved, and smiled what she hoped was an easy, casual smile but was concerned that she looked like a tortured hyena. Easy and casual had been alien to her recently. Her face felt tight and awkward, but thankfully he didn't seem to notice.

"Casey. Oh my God. I've been so worried about you," he said as he sat opposite her. "Are you okay?"

"I've been better, but I'm okay. What's everything been like at work?" she asked, half making small talk, and half wanting to know that they were panicking.

"Everything's completely normal. The first day, an email went around asking everyone to contact security if they heard from you, but that's it really."

Worry poked her stomach. After all they'd been through, she'd been sure that they would be packing up, cleaning databases, preparing for the worst. She'd never felt more like an insignificant gnat on the face of a giant organization.

Malcolm grabbed her untouched bottle of beer and took a swig from it. He opened his mouth to say something as the door swung open. Two men walked in together, and then sat at opposite ends of the bar.

Even for a nobody like Casey, it looked super-suspicious. She also realized that they could come to the booth and they'd be stuck there. "Did you tell anyone you were coming here?" she asked in a low voice. "Tell me now if you did, it's okay." It wasn't even slightly okay.

He looked shocked. "No, of course not. I don't want to get fired."

She tipped her head and looked at him in bewilderment. He really didn't get what was going on, despite the fact that he must know what was happening to her because he was the one who alerted her to James Turner's death. Nevertheless, she believed him. "Did anyone follow you here?" she asked.

"How would I know that?" He frowned.

Suddenly there was a small scream and both she and the table were drenched in beer. "Ee so sorry. So sorry." The wasted model in black had been on her way to the bathroom at the back and had stumbled and trashed them with her drink. Shit. She guessed a low profile was out of the question now.

A waitress came over and insisted they move to a different table. Casey took the opportunity to select a table in the middle of the bar, which was where she should have sat in the first place.

After they sat down again, the waitress bought napkins for her to dry herself off, and a free basket of chips and gua-camole. Kind of a score there. Maybe everything was going to go their way that evening after all.

She causally looked around the restaurant. The two men were gone, and Cameron—she was supercareful not to make eye contact—was just about resume his spot on a stool at the bar. Great time for him to decide he needed a bathroom break.

She turned her attention back to Malcolm. "Did you bring the drive?"

"Yeah. But why didn't you ask me for it this afternoon? Why did you ask me to meet you and then not show? That cost me over sixty dollars in taxi fares." He frowned.

"Sixty...what?" She didn't want to be a dick, but he was the VP of tech development and she was the VP of marketing. Their salaries couldn't be that different. Sixty dollars wouldn't have made a dent in her walking-around cash. "How much do you earn a year?" she asked, suddenly worried.

"You know we're not allowed to talk about our salary," he said, grabbing a handful of chips.

"No seriously." She feared what he was going to say.

"I'm on the same as all the VPs—three-seventy-five plus bonuses, which usually take it up to about half a mill, give or take. But I have a lot of student debt." His tone bordered on petulant.

"Same," she said, lying through her teeth. She couldn't muster the brain power to decide if it was better for him to be calm, or to be angry at his company. Casey earned about double his basic salary, and her first bonus had pretty much funded her entire retirement. Had they been trying to "buy'" her? Or to make her totally dependent on them? "I'll give you the sixty dollars, no problem."

He nodded, and then fell off his chair. Instantaneously, she recognized the muffled whizzing sound of a silencer. They'd shot him? White hot adrenaline spiked in her. She dropped to the sticky bar floor beside him. Malcolm was alive, but bleeding from his stomach. She tried to look to see where the shot had come from. She trusted that Cameron was dealing with it, but she still pushed the table over to shield Malcolm and herself from the bar area.

As she did she saw Cameron punching a guy at the bar. The other patrons had either run for the door or were cowering under their tables. This was bad.

The model was still slumped over her drink at the bar, gazing at it before taking a long sip. Probably just as well she was too drunk to panic. Cameron had his weapon out and was pointing it at her. What?

Several men in black came from the rear of the bar. She tried to nod Cameron over to them, but he kept his gun trained on her. And then she realized.

A hand snaked around her neck and dragged her up off the floor. It was the huge man she'd shot twice. She grabbed at the arm around her throat. Cameron's jaw clenched. In the mirror behind the bar, she could see her captor, face utterly impassive as she wriggled against him. His arm just tightened around her neck. This was it. First her shoulders prickled, and then her arms went numb. Blood was slowing as her heart slowed. Her toes ached. She struggled against him, but her feet were off the floor and she had no purchase to use.

Shit. Oh fuck. The model was on the move again. The woman's head dropped forward, she staggered toward the ladies' bathroom, but again, dropped her bag on the floor. She hiccoughed and giggled, and Casey could only watch in horror as she stood up, directly between Casey and Cameron. He no longer had a shot.

The model gave a sharp intake of breath, as the strap of her dress fell down her shoulder, exposing her breast to Casey and the man who was slowly killing her.

The arm across her throat loosened dramatically. He was obviously looking at the woman's perfectly formed breast, but Casey wasn't, because she had seen a shiny gun in the model's hand.

Casey pulled the man's arm away from her and dropped to the ground. The model shot him and he fell to the ground behind Casey. She looked to see if he was dead. There was a hole right in the middle of his forehead.

She looked around at the woman, who had jumped behind the upturned table. "Is your friend okay?" she asked, nodding toward Malcolm while pulling up her dress strap.

"He's alive, but he needs an ambulance," she replied.

"One's already on the way. Here." She shoved a small gun that she took from a thigh holster into Casey's hands. "Eyes up. There are four more guys about to breach the front door."

"Who *are* you?" Casey said, checking the rounds in the little weapon.

"Jack. Randy sent me to help."

"Jack." She remembered Randy calling "Jack." "You are not exactly how I imagined," she said.

"I get that a lot." She pulled back the slide on her gun and charged it again.

Three more guys appeared in tactical gear from the rear. "Are they police or TGO?" Casey asked, ready to put her hands up and surrender if they were the police.

Jack shot one in the leg. None of his colleagues even looked at him as he went down. The police would have dragged their colleague to safety. "TGO."

Cameron leapt into the fray like a freaking action star. He dispatched the two remaining men without using his weapon.

Jack shot three of the men who stormed through the window of the bar, not the door, as they'd expected. Casey dropped the last.

And then there was silence except for the canned Mexican music playing in the background. Cameron, Jack, and Casey stood and surveyed the carnage of broken glass, terrified patrons, and upturned furniture.

Cameron strode over to Casey and wrapped her in his arms. A mess of emotions flooded through her. Ones that she couldn't put a name to, or was afraid to.

"You'd better get going," Jack told them.

"Who *are* you?" Cameron asked.

"I'm Jack. Randy sent me to help you. He's been listening in on your calls." She bobbed her head a little, as if in concession. "Basically, he low-jacked you." She held up her hands. "Take it up with him. I just follow orders."

"Thank you," Casey said. "Your breast saved my life."

"If I had a dime…" Jack said with a grin. "Sorry for giving you an eyeful. It was the first thing I could think of." She put a finger to her ear, and listened to what was now obviously an earpiece. "The ambulance and police are two blocks away. You have to go. I'll stay and make sure Malcolm gets to the hospital."

Casey bent down to her friend. "How are you doing?" she asked, sweeping his floppy hair out of his eyes.

"I've been better," he said in a pretty clear voice, considering he'd been shot. "Here." He pressed a thumb drive into her hand. "I looked at it today for the first time. I didn't program any of that. I mean. I did. But they altered a bunch of my code."

"I'll look at it. Thank you. *Thank you.* I'll come see you in the hospital."

"Whatever," he said. "Wait. Do you think I can sue TGO for shooting me?"

"I think we both can. In fact, I have no doubt we might be able to get a class-action suit if we look back a few years. Pilots, researchers, us. A lot of people died at TGO's hands. I'm sure of it."

They bolted away from Al Chile's before the cavalry descended, and decamped to a parking lot on the Jefferson Davis Highway where Casey told him that she used to park to go for a morning run.

"There's one thing left we can do, now that we've got these." She waved both external drives in front of her face, as if she couldn't quite believe she'd got them. "Call the reporter who'd left her number with Biddy."

Cameron was silent. He didn't like putting their lives in the hands of a journalist. "I still think we need to see someone at the Pentagon—someone who can actually do something with this." He drummed his fingers on the steering wheel. As he said the words, he knew they sounded hollow.

Reporting it to the Pentagon would ensure the right people saw it, for sure. But it didn't mean anything would be done with the information. Maybe the government would walk away from the contract—and that was a big maybe—and save lives, but they would also be free to liquidate TGO and reopen as an entirely different entity, just as they had when James Turner had tried to shut them down.

Casey turned to him with a glimmer of a smile. "To be honest, it sounds as if you're trying to convince yourself rather than me."

"I am. Going to the media is just nothing—"

"I know. It's nothing you've ever had to contemplate before. But look. She's not a tabloid reporter, she's a White House correspondent. Anyway, this is a few years old. Probably the number won't work. Maybe in the morning we can call *Vanity Fair*'s corporate offices, see if we can get hold of her. And if it is her phone, then I can leave a message, and hopefully she'll call back in the morning, assuming she remembers meeting Mrs. Turner."

Really it was just another shot in the dark, but he nodded at the cell phone on the center console of the car. "Well, go ahead. Leave your message and we'll go find somewhere far away from here to stay. God only knows what the DC police are thinking right now. I wouldn't be surprised if we were on CNN again," he said. What had his life come to?

Casey carefully input the number from the card. The line rang, and then someone picked up. She looked startled. "Um, is this Grace Grainger's phone?"

The person on the other end answered in the affirmative. One curt word.

"Um, my name is Casey Jacobs, a woman called Biddy Turner—"

She was interrupted again, and Casey's puzzled gaze met his. "Yes, we're in DC. Okay. Okay. Yes. We'll see you there."

"Who's 'we'?" She repeated the question, looking with raised eyebrows at Cameron.

Jesus fucking Christ. He nodded. His career was over anyway. Besides which, their names had been on CNN.

"I'm with Colonel Duke Cameron—he's the commander of—"

She was interrupted again.

"Okay, we'll see you in five minutes." She hung up and he turned on the engine.

"I guess she's working late? Are we going to her office?" he asked, slipping the car into drive.

"No, she wants us to go to her home," Casey said with a frown. She gave him the address and directed him onto the highway again.

"So why do you look so worried?" he asked.

"It just seemed a little easy." She stared out of the window, and he realized how many times in the past week that he'd looked at her staring out of the window. Their whole relationship had taken place in a fucking car, pretty much. His mouth twitched as he remembered a part of the relationship that had happened *on* the car.

"This is it," she said, pointing at what looked like a four-floor brownstone. "No here…no back there…where are you—"

"Really, we have to go through this again?" he asked with a grin. He parked a few houses away.

They got out of the car, and moved really slowly toward the house. It suddenly felt as if every step he took would be taking Casey farther away from him. His gut told him that it all ended here, at this house. And then what?

# CHAPTER 18

Grace Grainger opened the door. She was petite, with shoulder-length dark hair. "Casey?" she asked.

"Yes, and this is Colonel Cameron," she said.

"Good to meet you, Colonel," Grace said sticking out her hand.

She closed the door behind them, and took a breath. "Right, where do we start?"

Before either of them could answer, a tall man came down the stairs, pulling on a tan T-shirt. Casey frowned. That was a military undershirt, and his body was whoa. It was as if he'd taken up the whole stairwell.

"This is my husband, Josh Travers," Grace said.

He stuck his hand out to Grace. "Ma'am," and then to Cameron. "Colonel. Good to see you. I'm from the Eighth Recovery Squadron. Now at the Pentagon."

"You're a pararescuer?" Cameron asked.

"Yessir." He caught both their gazes in turn. "So is this

it? Could this be the end of my wife's crusade? She's been working on this nearly every day—and night—for almost two years." He wrapped his arm around her shoulders. "I've missed her." He kissed the side of her head.

Casey's heart warmed at the sight of Grace's blush.

Josh squeezed Grace to him, then released her. He looked at Cameron.

"Where did you park, sir? The parking spaces are allocated here, so you can park right outside out house."

Cameron hesitated, and then grinned. "Probably best I don't. It's a stolen car."

Josh and Grace barely missed a beat. They looked at each other and said "The Evanses?"

Josh chuckled and took the keys from Cameron, who pointed out their car.

While they were on the stoop, Grace took Casey into a room on the second floor. Along with what looked like a bathroom, it was the only room on that floor. They walked in, and Grace switched on the light. Casey stopped breathing for a second. And then tears came. She sat on the red sofa, which was the only place to sit in the room. Sobs racked through her body. She covered her face with her hands. She couldn't process...

"Out of my way," she heard Cameron bellow. He burst into the room, making both Grace and Casey jump. His gaze rested on Casey for a second, and then accusingly at Grace. Then he saw what had caused Casey's tears.

The whole wall opposite the sofa was covered in TGO articles, photos of the board—including her—and blueprints, bank statements…the rest she'd have to get up to examine. But this was everything. Someone else knew what she knew. Someone else had investigated TGO. Someone else understood, and would believe her. The relief had just flooded out of her.

"Are you okay?" Cameron said, dragging his eyes from the wall to look at Casey.

"Just relieved. Just, really, really relieved." She couldn't stop the tears.

Grace handed her a tissue box. "I've been investigating TGO since a business reporter I knew wrote an absurd puff piece about them. I'd known him for years, and he'd been fired from a national paper for taking bribes to talk up companies that were floating on the stock exchange.

"So, right then, I pretty much knew something was up. But why would a military contractor need a PR boost in a national journal when all of the military companies were making money hand over fist? So, I started digging and found a product test on a missile had killed two technicians. And then I just kept digging, and the more stones I lifted up, the more powerful worms appeared. I knew something was wrong, I just didn't know what exactly.

"I wrote a couple of mildly critical articles, hoping it would flush out someone who knew something. And James Turner contacted me. A week later, he died on the day we were supposed to meet." She paused to take a breath. "I'm sorry." She looked at the wall again. "I've just been living this for a couple of years. And waiting for someone like you to call. I've been watching the news, and when they claimed you had something to do with the Red Flag crash, I figured you'd found something too." She raised her eyebrows expectantly.

Casey produced the two drives. "This is the one James Turner hid—his mother gave it to us yesterday…today?" She looked confusedly at Cameron, who shrugged. "And this I just got from a friend at TGO. He got shot about an hour ago."

"Oh my God, is he okay?" she asked, reaching for a notebook and pen.

"I think so," she said. "I think TGO has been selling hardware and software to our military. But they've been building back-doors into all the products and they've been selling the access to the back-doors to our enemies. Or just the highest bidder. The crash at Red Flag—I'm sure they did that deliberately. Either to show the back-door capability to a potential buyer, or to get rid of the pilots who may have realized what TGO was doing."

Cameron interjected. "We're on a time crunch. TGO signs a deal with NATO tomorrow. You know how government contracts work. Even if the project is canceled, TGO will still net billions."

Grace stopped scribbling and put her head down for a second. "I've got an idea," She said to Casey. "Fancy being an intern?"

James and Grace gave them the third floor of their house to stay in that night. They had planning to do, and after a flurry of calls to Randy and Captain Moss, a few overnight deliveries winged their way to Georgetown.

According to Captain Moss, Major Missy Malden had survived an attempt on her life, and the would-be murderer had killed himself in custody. The head of TGO's security, Chris Grove, had turned himself in, claiming that he was a lone wolf. Apparently he'd killed James Turner and others, without CEO Danvers even knowing. Danvers had disavowed Grove, but there was a strong feeling in the air force special investigations office that they were both lying. Cameron hoped that by tomorrow evening, they'd all be arrested.

Despite the wish that Cameron had contemplated when he'd last been in the shower with Casey, when they eventually got into bed, he didn't want to seduce her, to make love to her for hours. What he wanted was so fucking much more, but he didn't know how to tell her, or even if he should. They had a big day ahead of them, and what would happen after that was anyone's guess.

He held her in his arms, spooning around her body, trying to imprint every part of her in his mind, in case they went their separate ways.

"What happens now?" Casey asked him, after they'd been lying there for a little less than an hour.

"We've got a plan. As long as we follow that tomorrow—"

"No." She turned around. "Afterward. Us."

Her face was open and innocent to him, despite the fact that she'd been carrying heavy secrets and had killed people in the previous few days. And she was talking about having a tomorrow.

"I don't know," he parried, needing her to lead. They'd been through so much in the past few days. In reality, they'd only just met, but he had realized that basically they were the same person. They both had the same sense of justice, of service. They had the same sense of humor—although humor had been short on the ground. He was older than she was, but he had come to an understanding with himself, that retiring wasn't in the cards for him, and neither was returning to command Red Flag.

What was going to happen next *for them*. She had to decide that, because he already had a plan for them. But he didn't have the words to tell her what he wanted, what he felt. The feeling he had for her was a part of his breathing self. But the words. The words felt alien. He'd never used the words *love* or *forever* to anyone.

"I'm going to see if I can work for Randy," she said. "I should probably return everything he gave us…and the way we burned through his cash, I may have to work for him for a while before it's paid off," she said to his amazement. "I think you should take retirement from the air force and then come work with us."

His heart rate ticked up, the way it never did when he was on a mission. "What are you saying?" he said carefully.

She sat up. "I guess my plan is for you to work at Nellis until you retire and then go work for Randy. I'll have been working for him for a couple of years, so it's possible that I'd be your boss by the time you join…"

He tickled her and she wriggled away. "I'd take orders from you any day. I'm a hundred percent cool with that." He hesitated. Everything she'd said was about work. And then he decided to take charge of this so there were absolutely no misunderstandings. "And we'll do the long-distance thing?"

She frowned. "Sure. Except I'll lay bets that Randy'll let me fly to Nellis to see you. I'm sure it will be less a long-distance thing, and more of a long weekends thing." She sat up slightly. "I won't work there if I can't be with you too."

Everything inside of him flooded with warmth and light. It was a feeling totally alien to him. He pulled her toward him, so he could kiss her, but she pulled back.

"So, it's a plan then?"

"Just like that?" he asked skeptically, although his heart was singing inside. A whole future had opened up before him. A future where he was fulfilling his professional capabilities, getting back in the field, working for Randy, and having a totally legit future with Casey.

She shrugged. "Just like that." She searched his eyes. "It's a good plan, right?"

"Sure, as long as Randy wants us," he said, wondering how hard he'd have to push him for a job.

"He already does. I ran it past him when we talked on the phone." She searched his eyes again. "Are you mad?"

"Not even a little bit." He held her face, and kissed her, feeling a part of him disappear into her. She was his, and he was hers, and he'd never felt more peaceful.

# CHAPTER 19

It felt like the whole world was on the Capitol steps waiting for the press conference to start. Casey could see Danvers, smiling and shaking hands with various senators and congressmen. They were all waiting for the vice president to arrive before the conference that would lay out the terms of the contract TGO was about to sign.

Grace was at the front of the press gaggle, chatting to a couple of her colleagues. Cameras and really bright lights lit the podium where the speakers were going to be.

A man with an earpiece ran across the steps to Danvers. Casey watched the exchange carefully. Danvers nodded several times, then took the podium.

"Ladies and gentlemen of the press, Mr. Speaker of the House, senators, congressmen and -women, thank you for braving the cold DC morning to celebrate with us. Unfortunately, the vice president has been delayed, so we will proceed without him."

A shiver pulsed through Casey. What if the VP knew what was going to happen here? What if they'd all been tipped off? She hoped it was just a coincidence that was keeping the VP away that morning. She tried to shake it off. She was becoming paranoid.

There was a smattering of applause from those who were there to support TGO.

He continued. "We're here to celebrate the culmination of years of research and development that my company has undertaken to further the might and capability of the United States military."

There was more applause, and then Grace cut in. "Mr. Danvers. Is it accurate to say that you are a true patriot, one who loves the military?"

Casey noticed that there was a TV light shining on her too.

"Well, I wasn't going to take questions until the end, but I'm happy to answer that one. Yes, yes, I am a great supporter of the military."

"Then can you explain why you sent a TGO Syntec 8000 attack drone after Casey Jacobs and Colonel Duke Cameron—two people you are on record blaming for the accident at Red Flag?"

Danvers's face dropped for a microsecond, but then he rallied. "I'd explain that by saying that young reporters can be very gullible." He smiled down condescendingly at her.

The other reporters murmured in dissent. "Ms. Grainger has a Pulitzer Prize for journalism, Mr. Danvers," a man with an ABC microphone said with a frown.

"So, you're denying that a team of TGO security employees tried to kill Casey Jacobs in the parking lot of La Quinta hotel in Las Vegas, and then that they tried to run both her and decorated war hero Colonel Duke Cameron off the road, and then sent a TGO drone to shoot them?"

"I—er. I—of course I deny it. This is ridiculous. You have no proof." He looked around him for support, but it seemed to Casey that most of his "supporters" had literally taken a step back from him.

"You're right, she doesn't." Cameron's voice came from the rear of the reporter huddle. He cut a swathe through the reporters, cleanly shaven, looking sharp in his uniform, with its medals glinting in the cold sun.

"Who are you?" Danvers blustered, squinting into the morning sunlight. "I can't see…"

"Colonel Duke Cameron from Nellis Air Force Base. I'm sure you remember me from the control room, when we listened to the crash happening in real time? We heard the static, and the pilots report that their aircraft were uncontrollable. You didn't mention anything about your PreCall technology, and the back-door access you were willing to sell to the Russians." As he reached the front of the press pool, he threw the remains of the drone on the Capitol steps before Danvers. "And that is the drone that fired upon Casey Jacobs, shooting her twice."

Casey grinned as reporters turned their backs on Danvers and started speaking in urgent tones straight into their cameras.

"This doesn't prove anything. You could have bought this

from Radio Shack," Danvers protested, clearly unused to being challenged.

Casey took a deep breath. "But I have proof," she called
from the crowd. Danvers frowned and tried to figure out
who had spoken. Then he saw her and started to stutter
into the mic. "How did you…who? No. She's nobody." He
pointed at her. "Arrest her. She's responsible for the
crashes…She's not allowed here—this is a secure event."

Grace indicated the pass around Casey's neck. "She's my
intern. She's allowed here."

The reporter from ABC shoved his mic in her face. "Proof
of what?" he said.

Casey glared at Danvers. "I have proof that TGO has deliberately put back-doors into all the products it is about
to sell to NATO countries, and it has already started to
sell access to those back-doors to our enemies." She turned
to the ABC reporter. "James Turner realized what Danvers
was doing. He died trying to bring this into the open. He
died trying to protect our country. James Turner is the hero
today." That was for Biddy. She hoped that Biddy was watching.

The press gaggle got louder and louder, mics and cameras
swung around, and anchors spoke feverishly to people at the
studio.

Danvers started backing away from the podium, then
turned to run.

Casey shouted as loud as she could over the cacophony
"He's running!" Oh God, he couldn't get away. She'd be
looking over her shoulder forever.

And then it looked like he fell, but from the center of the press crowd she couldn't see. She pushed her way to the front, and saw Cameron climbing off her CEO's back, while a uniformed police officer arrested Danvers. He'd tackled him. Her hero, again.

# EPILOGUE

Eight months later, Casey was back in DC. Despite their best-laid plans, Cameron had not been able to ride out his retirement at Nellis. Instead, he'd been stuck in the capital, working on behalf of the Office of Special Investigations, which was digging in deep to find every compromised public figure, military officer, and to pull every loose strand of financing.

So far there had been thirty-six resignations from all three branches of the government, and both parties. Danvers had been sitting in jail, along with Chris Grove, who had eventually turned on Danvers to avoid spending the rest of his life in a cell.

Casey had come to DC to attend the final Senate committee meeting, where Cameron had been testifying. She stood in the corridor outside the room, waiting for the sergeant at arms to permit certain members of the public in to listen to the final testimonies. As he opened the door,

Casey was distracted by a group of people running down the corridor.

She frowned, and then recognized them. Major Missy Malden and her husband, Colonel Conrad; Major Eleanor Daniels, who had been required to give evidence against her own father; and her fiancé, the recently retired RAF pilot Flight Lieutenant Dexter Stone—the pilots who had crashed in the desert.

"I'm so happy you could make it," Casey said as they slowed down. She looked at the women who had been attacked by TGO, and the men who had supported them and fought alongside them. Although the toll TGO had taken on everyone was pretty big, the side effect of TGO's treasonous activities had been good. Three couples and one baby-on-the-way: Major Malden had told Casey that she was expecting when she'd invited them up for the final day's statements.

They filed into the committee room and took seats at the front of the public area.

Many of the people in the room had had to kill people in order to stay alive—including her. And regardless of their training, that changed people forever. Once the adrenaline had settled, it was too easy to second-guess the choices that had been made in a split second. For Casey it had been in a grocery store when she'd been buying milk.

A tall man had come up behind her to grab a two-gallon jug of milk, and she'd nearly attacked him. And then she cried, and then she'd called Eleanor. They'd become a support network for one another. And it seemed to have given them all strength.

As far as Casey was concerned, she just wanted Cameron back. Back in sight. Back in her bed. She breathed easier even as he entered the committee room and took the table in front of the senators who were there to finalize the investigation.

After thirty minutes of questions, Cameron was asked to give a final statement. He looked around at Casey, and the people sitting around her. Her heart clenched. She was so close to being alone with him again.

"The investigation took seven months. It is complete now. The summary is as follows. There have been thirty-six resignations and fifty-eight arrests on charges that range from murder to acceptance of bribes. TGO's operations have been shut down, and sixteen U.S. companies have filed to collaborate on a program that will assist the military in combatting the back-door advantage TGO had already sold to Russia and North Korea. Eighty-eight NATO aircraft and ships have been retrofitted to remove any TGO technology. The FBI has ongoing investigations into several individuals, but separate from our investigation. I submit this, my final report, respectfully, to the committee." Cameron indicated a large stack of papers compiled on a nearby table.

The ranking senator looked up and down the semicircle of committee members, who all nodded. "Thank you, Colonel. I declare this committee investigation closed, and you are dismissed."

Tears popped into Casey's eyes as she watched Cameron

stand and the senators leave the room. Eleanor grabbed her arm. "It's really all over. I never imagined it would happen. Half of me expected that they'd find a way to cover this all up."

"I know. I was too. But Cameron promised he wouldn't let it happen. And with Grace Grainger pushing the story constantly in the media, they really had no choice but to let the pieces fall."

They all stood and hugged one another. "Drinks?" Dex Stone asked.

"Hell, yeah," Conrad said. "We can drink to my daughter!"

Missy rolled her eyes, but her hand went instinctively for her belly.

They arranged to meet at Bipartisan Measures, a bar that Eleanor knew.

Casey waited for Cameron to come back out from the ante room he and the senators had disappeared into. He emerged, and his shoulders slumped a little when he saw her. "I have never been happier to finish a project," he said, wrapping his arms around her. "I've never been happier to see anyone in my life. I've missed you." He squeezed her.

"Are you coming back with me?" She'd flown in on one of Randy's aircraft.

"Of course. Now this is over, I'm never going to be on the opposite side of the country from you. It's too far. Too many time zones. Too many lonely nights." He grinned at her. "Besides, it'll give us at least five hours to negotiate our rules of engagement. I mean, if we're going to live together, we need to get some things straight. You know, bathroom schedules, division of chores, timeline for the wedding, who takes the trash out—that kind of thing."

Oh yeah, he was funny, but only she could see the uncertainty in his eyes. She knew he'd never say the words, and that was okay, he never had to with her. Her heart swelled, and she blinked tears from her eyes again. "Everything's negotiable, Cameron. You've just got to sell me on what you're bringing to the table."

He put his arm around her and walked her out of the committee room. "Every day, sweetheart. Every day."

# ABOUT THE AUTHOR

Emmy Curtis is an editor and a romance writer. An ex-pat Brit, she quells her homesickness with Cadbury Flakes and Fray Bentos pies. She's lived in London, Paris, and New York, and has settled for the time being in Germany. When not writing, Emmy loves to travel with her military husband and take long walks with their dogs. All things considered, her life is chock-full of hoot, just a little bit of nanny. And if you get that reference... well, she already considers you kin.

Learn more at:
EmmyCurtis.com
Facebook.com/EmmyCurtisAuthor
Twitter @EmmyCurtis19

www.ingramcontent.com/pod-product-compliance
Ingram Content Group UK Ltd.
Pitfield, Milton Keynes, MK11 3LW, UK
UKHW022256280225
455674UK00001B/53

9 781478 947981